"What . . . " She cleared the huskiness out of her throat. "What do you usually do when you get in this condition?"

With one finger he tipped her chin up so she was again looking him in the eyes.

"Take a long, cold shower," he said solemnly, and then he kissed her.

As kisses went, Carly thought dazedly, this one would knock the you-know-what out of the Richter scale.

She was melting in his arms like a piece of chocolate left out in the sun, and the knowledge frightened her. "Chase," she whispered, opening her eyes again; "I—I don't think this is such a great idea."

"Why not?" he whispered back. "It feels pretty great to me."

She moaned and tilted her head back. "You . . . we're . . . I'm not . . . " The thoughts flitted around her head like elusive, dancing butterflies on a summer afternoon. She chased them, but they darted away too quickly.

He pressed a fleeting kiss to her neck. "You're not what?"

"Very good at this," she said weakly.

"I hate to disagree with you, sweetheart," he said, "but you're *very, very* good at this."

WHAT ARE *LOVESWEPT* ROMANCES?

They are stories of true romance and touching emotion. We believe those two very important ingredients are constants in our highly sensual and very believable stories in the LOVE-SWEPT line. Our goal is to give you, the reader, stories of consistently high quality that may sometimes make you laugh, sometimes make you cry, but are always fresh and creative and contain many delightful surprises within their pages.

Most romance fans read an enormous number of books. Those they truly love, they keep. Others may be traded with friends and soon forgotten. We hope that each LOVESWEPT romance will be a treasure—a "keeper." We will always try to publish

LOVE STORIES YOU'LL NEVER FORGET
BY AUTHORS YOU'LL ALWAYS REMEMBER

The Editors

Loveswept 800

THE MATING GAME

RAEANNE
THAYNE

BANTAM BOOKS
NEW YORK · TORONTO · LONDON · SYDNEY · AUCKLAND

THE MATING GAME
A Bantam Book / August 1996

ISBN 0-553-44563-4

Published simultaneously in the United States and Canada

Bantam Books are published by Bantam Books, a division of Bantam Dou-
bleday Dell Publishing Group, Inc. Its trademark, consisting of the words
"Bantam Books" and the portrayal of a rooster, is Registered in U.S.
Patent and Trademark Office and in other countries. Marca Registrada.
Bantam Books, 1540 Broadway, New York, New York 10036.

PRINTED IN THE UNITED STATES OF AMERICA

OPM   0 9 8 7 6 5 4 3 2 1

ONE

Her hands fixed tight to the steering wheel, Carly Jacobs rotated her shoulders and tried to relax. Slipping and sliding along a precarious mud bog of a mountain road wasn't exactly the best way to unwind after the stressful two weeks she'd just been through, she decided, peering through the rain-spattered windshield. The murky darkness was only barely illuminated by the twin beams of her headlights.

"This has got to be one of your brainier ideas, Carly," she said aloud. "Right up there with cutting your own hair in second grade and nearly marrying Phillip Bainbridge."

At least she was in one of the big state Broncos, instead of her own small pickup, she thought. Her new boss at the Wyoming Game and Fish Department had insisted she take it, since she'd be patrolling for fishing violations tomorrow.

She chuckled as she remembered her conversation with Verl Handley, supervising warden, who'd known her since she was considered the wildest urchin to menace the streets of Whiskey Creek. He'd told her, in a tone that brooked no argument, that she would be completely worthless if she had to spend another weekend with her mother.

"Take the truck," he'd said. "Get away from Betsy and spend a little time up in the mountains. Maybe that will settle you down, so you're not as high-strung as a filly bedded with a rattler."

He'd been right, Carly thought. After two weeks with her well-meaning, but infinitely exhausting, mother, she was ready to start tearing out her hair, strand by strand. A twenty-seven-year-old woman, used to wondrous independence, could only take so much fluttery pampering. Moving to her family's cabin outside of town would have to be accomplished this weekend if she wanted to retain any kind of hold on her sanity.

Come hell, or in this case, high water, she was going to settle in.

As if to mirror her thoughts, the back wheels on the big vehicle suddenly began to spin. Carly swore under her breath while she steered into the skid, then tried to muscle the vehicle back onto the road. The only sound in the moonless night was her own nervous breathing and the whine of the four-wheel drive as she downshifted to second gear to aid her traction.

When the truck caught solid ground again, she blew out her breath in relief and risked a glance in the rearview mirror. Her redbone hound was still stretched out on the backseat, snoring gently.

"You're a real pal, Jackson," she muttered, grinning

as the hound sniffled and turned onto his back. "You're missing the best part of the drive, you lazy mutt."

In daylight, this area would be breathtaking. Giant lodgepole pine towered alongside the road, their fringy branches forming a dark green tunnel that blocked all but a smattering of sunlight from sneaking through. A blue-ribbon trout stream slithered beside the dirt road, and in the distance she would have been able to see the rough, snow-dusted peaks of the Wind River mountain range.

But on this Friday night in early June, all Carly could see was slick mud, ominous shadows, and the occasional brave deer browsing on the side of the road.

The silence in the Bronco only intensified her jitters, allowing her to listen to the sundry anxieties of her overactive imagination. Music. That's what she needed.

She only glanced down for a moment, just long enough to turn the radio on, hoping to find some station that could thrust its signal through the mountains and trees. But when she returned her attention to the road, she gasped and braked hard at the sight that greeted her. The Bronco slid out of control just long enough for her breath to catch before the vehicle shuddered to a jerky stop scant feet from a wet, mud-covered figure, tall and menacing in the dim light.

Carly slammed her eyes shut. Maybe it was a trick of the shadows or her headlights reflecting off a puddle. She cautiously opened one eye, then the other, then felt a shiver skid across her shoulders. Nope. The hulking figure was still there, all right, looking otherworldly, an apparition yanked from a child's nightmare and shoved into her world.

Didn't the guys at work say that a rancher over in Pinedale had reported some of his sheep gone and giant footprints leading into the mountains? Maybe she was face-to-face with Sasquatch. Bigfoot. Yeti. Whatever the heck the Wyoming version was called. She shivered again. All the childhood tales her older brother used to taunt her with about wicked beasties who carry off naughty little girls jostled across her mind, and she urgently checked the locks on the doors.

"Jack, wake up," she said. "What does that look like?" The dog obliged her by plopping his chin on the back of her seat and peering through the window. He looked at her quizzically, barked once, then settled back down to his doggy dreams.

Okay, so it wasn't Bigfoot. Either that, or her hound didn't have a protective bone in his body.

No. She caught a silver reflection off to the side of the road. No, not Bigfoot, unless all your better mythological creatures were driving luxury sedans these days.

The car, its wheel wells covered in muck, was nose-first in the brush, its elegant rump sticking onto the road. A wave of relief washed away all her bogeyman imaginings, replacing them with derision, both at herself and at whatever idiot would bring a car like that out on a night like this. It was probably one of the greenhorn Rolex-and-caviar guests at the Lazy Jake Lodge, she thought scornfully.

She rolled down her window. "Hello," she called, watching the figure move toward her with a peculiar rolling gait, almost a limp. Something about the mud-covered man—and she could tell by the breadth of the shoulders that it was definitely a man—reminded her of someone. It was too dark, though, to determine whether she knew him.

"Hey," the figure called back genially, still five yards away. "Thanks for stopping. I've tried everything I can think of to pull the blasted thing out. I was just about ready to start for the lodge when I heard your truck around the bend."

Carly narrowed her eyes. His voice strummed along her spine and worked its way into her subconscious. She knew this man, no doubt about that. But how?

When he reached her truck, she saw his steely blue eyes, startling and bright in his muck-covered face, and her heart slammed hard in her chest. Her hands, clammy already from the strain of negotiating the hazardous road and her shock of a minute before, slipped on the steering wheel and she inhaled a few quick breaths.

Oh, yes. She knew this man. Chase Samuel-son—hometown hero, prematurely retired major league baseball star, successful businessman, and source of her hatred for ten years. He stood just a handshake away, all six feet two inches of him.

Personally, she would have preferred Bigfoot.

She battled down a panicky urge to roll the window up, put the truck back in gear, and head off into the darkness. It was too late anyway. Recognition flooded his eyes as he got a closer look at her.

"Carly? Carly Jacobs? Is that you?" He whistled, and she could see white teeth gleaming in the night as he grinned. "I can't believe it. Little Carly Jane is all grown up and driving a big boy state truck."

She gripped the steering wheel with suddenly nerve-less fingers. Why did it have to be Chase? She couldn't very well drive off, although spinning her wheels in his face would be immensely satisfying. The instinct, though compelling, contradicted any sense of decency she possessed. The lodge was more than three miles away, and the brutal frigid rain showed no signs of stopping.

It was also too dark to safely pull the Cadillac out of the mud, especially with the creek precariously close on the other side of the road, and conditions so slick.

She muttered another oath and looked up at him. He was still grinning, damn him.

"Get in," she managed to say. It wasn't hard to keep her voice completely free of cordiality, and she noticed with great satisfaction that he looked startled at her hostile tone.

"You don't have to take me so far out of your way," he said. "Why don't you just tow me out?"

She glared at him. "Because if, by some miracle, I manage to get you unstuck without taking an uncomfortably chilly dip in the creek, more than likely you wouldn't get two feet in this stuff without landing right back where you started."

He looked unconvinced, and she rolled her eyes. Heaven spare her from the male ego, she thought. And Chase certainly had more than his fair share.

"Get in, Chase, or I'll leave you here to wait for the next ride." Even he had to realize the prospects of any other vehicle traversing the lonely dirt road in the middle of a rainstorm were dim, at best.

He finally opened the passenger door and climbed in with the same grace that had given sportswriters fits of euphoria. Carly handed him a rag from the backseat to wipe off the mud. Driving off again, she watched him out of the corner of her eye while he rubbed the rag across his face, then swiped at his hands.

Bloody hell, she thought. He still was the most gorgeous male she'd ever seen, even in the weak light from the dashboard display. Strange, tingly goosebumps erupting on her skin told her that her traitorous body had noticed it too.

He'd grown a mustache since his days in the pros, a dark, bristly thing that gave him the appearance of an outlaw from the old Wild West. Dangerous. Forbidding. Intriguing. She blew out a little puff of air, willing her body to ignore him.

"It's great to see you, Carly." His voice echoed in the close confines of the vehicle, and she jumped in her seat, startled from the unwilling attraction she had no business feeling for him. "I hadn't heard you were back in Whiskey Creek," he continued. "How long will you be home?"

She fervently wished she could ignore him, that she could pretend she'd never made the mistake of stopping. But the twenty-minute ride would be excessively awkward if she went with her instincts.

"The Wind River district needed some extra hands for an investigation they've got going, so they borrowed me for a few months. I'll probably be going back to Cheyenne by Labor Day." She lapsed into stony silence again, hoping he would take the hint.

"So how've you been for the last ten years?"

No such luck. She scowled. "Like you said, it's been ten years, Chase. There've been a few ups and downs along the way." A lot more downs, thanks to him, than there should have been, she added to herself.

"Last I heard, you were gonna marry some rich city-boy lawyer from Laramie."

Carly gritted her teeth. "And last I heard, you were optioned by the Oakland A's after five seasons because your weak knees couldn't take the big leagues."

He chuckled at her retort, a rich, low, sexy sound that did annoyingly delicious things to her nerve endings, until she sternly reprimanded the beastly things.

"You might have grown up, but you certainly haven't changed completely, Snarly Carly. You always did know how to pitch to a man's weak spot."

Snarly Carly. She closed her eyes for the briefest of moments against the pain that soaked through her at that name. Only her brother and his best friend, Chase, had ever called her that.

Mike had coined the name for her. Not because of any bad attitude, although he used to tease her with the nickname until she retaliated with either a punch in the ribs or a swift kick to the shins. No, the name had stuck because of Betsy Jacobs's ridiculous insistence that her only girl look like one of those Barbie dolls she persisted in giving Carly every Christmas and birthday.

Her mother had staunchly refused to let Carly—who preferred bib overalls to pinafores and dump trucks to dollies—cut her curly blond hair. As a result, most of her girlhood had been spent with a frizzy cloud drifting around her head, usually adorned by grass and sticks and the occasional bug.

She almost laughed at the memory of Betsy's daily harangue, and at Mike's affectionate teasing, until she remembered Chase's presence in the truck. A queer tightness clutched at her chest, and she compressed her lips tightly.

She wouldn't give him the satisfaction of knowing he'd unnerved her.

"What brings you out on a nasty night like tonight?" she asked instead, in her crispest, official tone.

Chase blinked at the abrupt change of subject but didn't comment. "I landed in Jackson late this afternoon from a business trip to San Francisco. Since Pop didn't know exactly when I'd be back, I decided to rent a car so he wouldn't have to drive all the way there and back. It's just my dumb luck it happens to be monsoon season out here."

Dumb luck? What did he know about dumb luck? she wondered. The only kind of luck Chase Samuelson ever experienced was the golden kind. The kind of luck where talent scouts sign you out of the blue, the kind where women melt into a pile of hormones at your feet if you so much as quirk a dimple at them.

The kind of luck where old friends don't have to matter.

"It's been raining for a week," she said quietly, tonelessly, hands white from the effort it took to appear calm.

"It looks like it. Still, we need the rain." He paused for a moment. "Carly, I'm sorry about your dad's death last year. Whiskey Creek lost the best principal it's ever had and a damn good man."

She nodded her head in acceptance.

"I was out of town, or I would have come to the funeral to pay my respects."

You're real good at missing funerals, aren't you, Chase?
The taunt hovered on her tongue, acid and mean, and
she quickly swallowed it. The time to bring up Mike and
all the pain that lay between them was definitely not
when she had her hands full with two-thousand pounds
of slippery truck.

"How's your grandfather?" she asked instead.

"Pop? A little rusty in the hinges, but he still rides
the rest of us into the dirt."

Again, she almost laughed, remembering the dear
old man who'd raised Chase and his sisters, but she
stopped herself just in time.

For several minutes, the silence stretched between
them, taut and stiff, like a guitar string too tightly
wound. He filled the interior of the Bronco like a hand
in a snug leather glove, and she couldn't help being
jolted into awareness each time he moved. She couldn't
see him well, but she could feel the heat emanating from
him, could hear the rustle of his jeans on the seat like a
roar in her ears.

Finally, in desperation as her imagination began to
paint a picture of just how, exactly, he filled those jeans,
she blurted out the first thought that came to her.

"How's Jessie?"

As soon as the two words left her mouth, Carly
squeezed her eyes shut for a second, chagrined and horrified at herself. The woman who had been the love of
her brother's too-short life was absolutely the last thing
she wanted to discuss with anyone, least of all the man
who had stolen her away from Mike.

"She's married to an accountant in Salt Lake City,"

Chase answered easily, "and they're raising two little geniuses."

He shrugged those massive, poster-boy shoulders, and she felt the vibration travel the length of the bench seat in a soft caress against the muscles in her back. "She seems happy enough," he added. "I'm glad. She deserves some happiness."

"Uh, great. That's just great. Good for her." Carly loosened her jacket and fumbled to turn down the truck's heater, against the blaze of heat that seemed to spring up from nowhere.

"Yeah, I run into her sister in town sometimes, and she tells me what's been going on. That famous Whiskey Creek grapevine lets me know just about everything that past and present residents have been up to. You'd be surprised what you can discover hanging out at RJ's Café."

His voice took on a teasing note, and Carly stiffened against its mesmerizing, snake-charmer effect, but not quickly enough. Somehow that deep voice managed to lull her into a calm, and she was completely unprepared for his next words.

"I'd heard, for instance, that Carly Jacobs had grown up into a beautiful woman, leaving broken hearts strewn across eastern Wyoming like so much sagebrush."

Startled, she turned her head to stare at him. *Dumb move, Carly*, she snapped to herself. He was watching her through half-closed eyes, and he stretched his arm along the seat to touch her cheek with his thumb. Then, ever so slowly, he dragged it down and cupped her chin with long fingers. The rough pads of his fingertips seemed to sizzle against her skin.

"Talk about an understatement," he said huskily, and Carly, shocked back into her senses, jerked her chin away. Her face flamed even hotter, and she took a shaky breath.

Boy, was she going to kill Verl for talking her into going to the cabin tonight!

"Don't believe everything you hear, Chase," she finally said. To her horror, her voice came out smoky and low. She cleared the gruffness away and tried again. "You and I both know that silly things like truth and reality don't hold much water when it comes to the good gossips around Whiskey Creek."

"I don't need gossips to tell me what kind of woman you've become," he answered.

Carly stared out the window in desperation and nearly burst into tears of relief when a familiar shape emerged through the dark pines, rough-hewn logs shiny-black in the rainy night. The Lazy Jake! Thank heavens!

She jerked the truck to a stop. "Well, here we are. I'm sure you can find somebody to take you back to the rental in the morning. If you ask me, you ought to either wait until the mud dries or get a tow back to town, rather than try to make it up here. Who knows how long this weather's going to keep up, and somebody might not happen along to pick you up the next time. Tell your grandpa hello for me and all that." Carly clamped her teeth together with a sharp click. Good grief, she was babbling like a teenager on her first date!

Chase just grinned, his even white teeth gleaming wolfishly as the moon emerged from behind the clouds. He climbed out of the truck, and Carly was about to

drive off as fast as the truck and Mother Nature would allow, when he walked around to her side of the vehicle.

"I'm glad you're home, Carly. I've missed you. Why don't we get together one of these nights and talk about our wayward past?"

"Our wayward past?"

"Sure. What else would you call it?"

Nightmare. One big horror movie. A taste of heaven, her honest inner self insisted. Again, memories crowded against her mind, piling at the door of her subconscious. Adventurous weekend camping trips the three of them took, before her mom prohibited her from going when she turned thirteen. Mike, Chase, and herself crowded into the backseat of her dad's car to travel four hundred miles to Denver for a Broncos game. Illicit midnight fishing trips that inevitably ended with Mike catching the biggest brookie and Carly getting dunked by the two of them.

Mike. Always Mike.

"I don't have anything to talk about with you, Chase," she answered sharply. "Nothing at all."

She started to roll the window up, but he used his hands to force it down. In the faint light from the lodge porch, she could see his jaw harden as he leaned closer.

"C'mon, Carly, sure you do." Anger glinted in his narrowed eyes, even though the words came out lightly. "You can tell me why you're being so nasty to me, for starters, why you flinch if I so much as look at you. And then maybe we can get into why you never used any of those plane tickets I sent you, just like I promised I would, so you could come watch a game. After that, we could chat about why you managed to avoid me every time I came home, before you left for college."

"Don't," she ordered, her throat tight with unshed tears.

"Don't what? Don't invite an old friend out for a beer some night? You're finally old enough to drink it."

"Don't make me out like I'm the one who hurt you!" She wanted nothing more than to open the door and fall into his arms as she'd done so often in an earlier life, to turn to Chase's strength for the comfort he'd always been more than willing to provide. She wanted to press her cheek against that broad chest, slide her arms around his waist, and hold on as tightly as she could, until she filled in the canyons of loneliness that had been carved by his absence from her life.

She checked the impulse with a harsh reminder of what lay between them.

"Whatever friendship we shared so long ago is gone, Chase. It died the day Mike did. Rehashing it wouldn't do anybody any good. I'm only going to be in town for a few months, so here's the deal. You just stay out of my way, and I'll make sure I stay out of yours." With luck, they wouldn't even run into each other during the summer.

As she rolled the window up, his soft laugh drifted across the wet air. "Not a chance in hell, Carly," she thought she heard him say. She pounded the steering wheel with her fist, then pulled away, not caring in the slightest that the spinning tires on the four-by-four spewed more wet earth onto Chase Samuelson. Maybe a little mud would wipe that damned arrogant smirk off his face.

———◈—————◈———

"Well, Miss Snarly Carly, you just try staying out of my way," Chase said aloud as he watched the red tail lights on the Bronco recede. "I've got a feeling we're going to see a whole lot more of each other than you're gonna be completely comfortable with."

He waited until the lights had blurred to a distant pink and finally vanished into the night. As he let the hard rain pelt the mud from his clothes, he couldn't help chuckling. The little tomboy who'd dogged the heels of her older brother and him had grown into one hell of a woman.

He tried to re-create her image in his mind. If only the light had been a little stronger, he thought wistfully. He'd caught fleeting impressions of that unforgettable curly blond hair caught back in a braid, with tendrils escaping to frame a face that had looked wraithlike, with eyes dominating her delicate features. He relied on memory to fill in the eye color—a warm cocoa shade that always used to make him think of settling into a big easy chair in front of a crackling fire.

He'd admitted to himself a long time ago that he was half in love with her back when they'd still been friends. At the time, the unwilling response he experienced whenever she was around had terrified him, disgusted him even. She'd been just a kid, fourteen to his eighteen, when he left town for college.

Despite the difference in their ages, and the fact that they'd practically grown up together, he'd been drawn to her for reasons that confounded him. She'd been a hellion as a teenager, a tomboy who rebelled against any kind of rules, who wore no makeup and defied her mother by cropping that luscious hair. Who relished telling every girl he dated about all his weaknesses, expounding at great length about how he couldn't pitch worth beans and had flunked kindergarten.

Chase laughed into the night. She hadn't succeeded in scaring off too many of them, but despite a fairly active social life, he'd never been able to shake his attraction to little Carly Jane.

Sorry, sweetheart, he thought. *I'm definitely not staying out of your way.* She'd fired his blood back then, and if their brief encounter tonight was any indication, she still had the same power. It was about time he found out if the fantasies that had been percolating in his subconscious could compare to flesh-and-blood reality.

A sudden wind, sharp with chill, whipped through his wet clothes, disturbing the flow of memories. Chase climbed the steps into the lodge and opened the huge oak door, meeting on the other side the welcoming scent of cinnamon-laced apple pie and intense heat generated by the massive stone fireplace taking up nearly one entire wall of the room.

A few boys and girls from one of the younger camp groups, all unfamiliar to him, sat on the rugged furniture grouped around the fireplace. They looked up as his entrance sent a gust of moist air inside to tease the fire into dancing shadows.

"Look what the cat dragged in," Elizabeth, one of his four camp counselors, teased.

"Hey, kids. Sorry I wasn't here when you arrived." He hated to miss their first day, but the outdoor training camp lasted for three weeks. He'd be able to spend more time with them in the next few days.

"That's okay, Mr. Samuelson," a little girl of about nine piped up.

"Have you guys had fun so far?"

"Uh-huh," a freckled redheaded boy said. "It's way cool. We took a horseback ride and we went on the canoes and we had fudge. It was awesome."

Chase knew that for most of these children, with their special problems, fudge was a rare treat indeed.

"I hope you saved me some."

The boy's face fell. "We didn't. Sorry, Mr. Samuelson."

"Call me Chase." He tousled the boy's hair. "Don't worry about the fudge. I'm sure I can rustle up something in the kitchen."

He started to mount the stairs, only to be met by his grandfather coming down.

"Son, what in blazes you doin' home so early?" Jake Samuelson, still fit and energetic at eighty, hurried down the long, curved staircase—the half-log steps he and Chase had painstakingly constructed the winter Chase was forced to come to terms with the premature end to his baseball career.

Jake crossed the hall and slapped Chase on the back. Chase pretended to stagger from the force of the greeting, just like he always did. His grandfather rolled his eyes, just like he always did.

"I thought I heard somebody pull up," Jake went on, "then I saw tail lights out the window. What damn fool did you con into givin' you a ride all this way?"

"I tried to rent a truck in Jackson, but all they had

left were luxury cars, and I ended up stuck in the mud a few miles down the road. Fortunately, Carly happened by in a state truck and she picked me up."

"Carly? Little Carly Jacobs?"

"Right." Not so little anymore. "Listen, I'm going to shower and change into something dry. Meet me in the kitchen and I'll tell you how the foundation's fund-raiser went."

A short while later, dressed in clean jeans and a warm blue sweatshirt, Chase poured himself a glass of milk and savored another taste of the crispy-crust Dutch apple pie.

"I swear, you're still tryin' to eat me out of house and home." Jake sauntered into the kitchen and pulled out one of the weathered old chairs that encircled the pine table.

The chairs had been there forever. Chase distinctly remembered sitting at this same table the night he and his two younger sisters, traumatized by a lifetime of hearing screaming fights and slamming doors, had been brought there to live with his father's parents.

It had been a rainy night like this one, Chase recalled, a night filled with more terror than an eight-year-old should have to deal with, leaving the only home he'd ever known to be dumped by his father on a wrinkled old couple he'd never even met. He still couldn't believe Jake and Alice had agreed to take responsibility for him and his younger sisters.

They had willingly opened their home and their hearts to the children in what was supposed to have been a temporary situation, just while their father made enough in the oil fields to buy a house for him and the children. But with the sad wisdom of the very young, Chase had known even then that his reckless father wouldn't come back. Now he could barely remember the mother who had run out on them or the father who had died a few years later in a drilling accident.

In all the ways that mattered, Jake and Alice had been their parents. When Alice had died eight years earlier from cancer, he and his sisters had mourned her as deeply as any children mourn a mother.

He grinned now at Jake, awash in tenderness for the old man. "I'm a growing boy, Pop. Would you begrudge your only grandson a little nourishment?"

Jake snorted. "I would when it's Louella's apple pie you're snarfin' down," he grumbled. "That sassy cook of yours says she's not makin' another one until fall when she can use fresh apples from out back."

Chase pointed with his fork to the counter, where he'd saved the last piece. Jake rubbed his hands together in glee and brought the pie over to the table. For a few minutes, they ate in companionable silence while Chase debated how to broach the subject of a brown-eyed slip of a woman who'd suddenly come barreling back into his life.

"Pop, tell me what you remember about Carly," he said finally.

"Little Carly?" Jake scratched his cheek, the raspy stubble catching on a thumbnail. "Not much. She works for the Forest Service or some such outfit . . ."

"Game and Fish," Chase interjected.

"That's right. Game and Fish." Jake shrugged. "I ran into Betsy a few weeks ago over to Al's Hardware and she said Carly ain't gettin' hitched to that lawyer fellow in Cheyenne, but she didn't tell me any details. She sure looked sad when she was talking about it, though. Mamas hate to see them lawyer types get away."

Chase knew about her job. He'd made it a point to know she'd excelled in college. He also knew she'd been hired by the state just after graduation, that she'd been tops in her class when she went through police officer training school to specialize in the law enforcement side of game management, that she'd lived in various parts of Wyoming since then.

Like he'd told her, the grapevine in small towns like Whiskey Creek could be surprisingly effective.

"What about before she left town?" he asked.

Jake took his time before answering. "That little gal was never the same after Mike died. She pined like I've never seen anybody pine. Damn near wasted away."

Chase tried to ignore the pinching guilt that always hit him at the mention of Mike. It wasn't his fault, he reminded himself, a litany he'd repeated countless in the last decade. There had been no alternative.

"He was her brother. She loved him," he said quietly, suddenly bleak.

"Yeah, I know. But it was more than that." A frown furrowed the web of wrinkles on Jake's leathery face. "She couldn't have been more than sixteen or seventeen, but all of a sudden she starts actin' like an old lady. She stopped goin' to any of them high school things, and didn't come over to see your sister anymore. You remember how she and Penny used to hoot and holler when they got together, but all that stopped when Mike died." Jake shuddered. "Kind of spooky, if you ask me, how a sweet young girl like that could just stop livin' for a while."

The refrigerator whirred, disturbing the distracted silence that had fallen between them, and Jake summoned a smile and changed the mood.

"Boy, she sure worshiped you two boys. She'd follow you around like she didn't dare let the two of you out of her sight. And she was the pluckiest gal I've ever seen. You 'member that time you all got lost up on Whitehorse Peak? You two boys musta been about thirteen and she was, what, about eight or nine? When we finally found you, there she was tellin' you jokes and laughin' like she hadn't a care in the world."

Chase took a swig of milk. He remembered. He and Mike had been terrified when they realized they'd taken a wrong turn after fishing one day, but they'd made a pact not to let Carly see how desperate their situation was. She'd kept on telling the jokes long after dark. Finally Mike, in his fear, had lashed out at her, telling her to shut her mouth for three seconds so they could figure out how to get home.

"You're so stupid you don't even know we're lost!" he'd shouted.

Carly had stared at her brother for a few seconds, then tossed her head. "Sure I do," Chase clearly remembered her sing-song little-girl voice saying proudly. "I was just tryin' to keep you guys from gettin' scared."

She'd then proceeded to point them in the right direction and skipped along behind—gabbing the whole way—while they followed the trail that eventually led to their rescue.

He shook his head to clear the image. That little girl

was gone now, replaced by a prickly woman who obviously blamed him for events that had been beyond his control. The trick would be proving his innocence without smashing completely whatever cherished memories she carried of her brother.

And then trying to spark the same desire in her that still coursed through him, one hour and a cold shower later.

Yep. It was going to be an interesting summer.

TWO

What a gorgeous day!

One hiking boot perched on the doorframe of the state truck, Carly drew a deep breath, inhaling the moist, sweet air remaining from the storm the night before.

As if to make amends for the constant deluge of the past week, Mother Nature had bestowed a sunny smile on western Wyoming.

Despite the splendor of the setting, Carly yawned, a big, wide stretch of her mouth that nearly popped her eardrums. She'd certainly experienced more restful nights, she thought ruefully, trying to shake the last vestiges of sleep from her fuzzy brain.

Coming to the family cabin was like confronting years of repressed memories. It was steeped in reminders of her childhood, of that golden time when she didn't have anything more pressing to worry about than how she could con Mike into letting her sleep in the top bunk in the loft they'd claimed as their own.

Phantom memories of her father and brother

haunted this place. She should have realized they would, that opening the door to the dwelling would send them tumbling against one another in a haphazard wrestling match.

Her family had spent every summer here that she could remember, in the little cabin at the edge of the great wilderness. This was where her father would write his stories that would remain forever unpublished; where her mother would cook and sew and, as she called it, "putter around"; and where she and Mike would push each other down the steps each morning in a rush to embrace whatever adventures the day would bring.

She'd spent the long, nearly sleepless night wrapped in blankets on the heart-pine floor, listening to the restless stirring of logs in the fireplace and the *ping* of rain hitting the tin roof.

And remembering.

The unfortunate encounter with Chase certainly hadn't helped the situation. Like the cabin, he was inexorably entwined with her family's history. If anything, seeing him had summoned up a whole host of feelings better left unexplored, not the least of which was the unholy mix of hatred and tenderness she felt toward him, underlined by a sexual attraction that both shocked and confused her.

Don't think about it, she advised herself now. It was some weird trick of the moonlight that made him look so beautifully familiar. Since she wasn't going to see him again anyway, maybe it would all disappear. Sort of like a bad case of poison ivy.

She forced her attention back to the alpine scene spread out before her. Drops of rain still clung to the deep green needles of the pines surrounding the cabin, and as she looked around an energetic gray squirrel bounced on a branch overhead, sending a shimmering shower onto her head. In reflex, she tilted her head up, and through the branches she caught sight of a hawk wheeling and dancing high above. Its piercing cry sent a shiver down her back.

Wyoming was a beautiful state. She knew it, because she'd been stationed in all four corners of it and had been lucky enough to see back country most people would never even hear about. Yet the Wind River far surpassed anything she'd seen in her travels.

Truth was, she'd always thought of the vast mountain range as her own personal playground, despite the thousands of people who visited it each year.

Jackson barked, eager for action, and Carly smiled. "I know, I know. We've got places to go, a river to patrol, nasty ol' lawbreakers to cite. And none of that's getting done while we stand here admiring the view."

She'd have all summer to do that. A whole long, lonely, introspective summer.

Ten hours later, sweaty and about ready to drop from exhaustion, Carly stopped at the last spot she needed to check on the Whiskey. The sun, now sending long slivers of shadow between the trees as it faded, had been merciless all day. Temperatures on what had started as a pleasant early summer day had rapidly soared, until it was just plain hot.

She cautiously touched the tip of her nose and winced at the sharp sting. She could just hear her mother now: "Carly Jane Jacobs, didn't I raise you with more sense than to spend all day in the sun without a hat? You're going to have skin cancer before you're thirty, mark my words!"

"Yes, I know, Mother," she spoke aloud to her imagination. "And die an ugly spinster in hiking boots, alone with my cats."

Jackson barked at her quizzically, then yawned and flopped onto his stomach in the backseat.

"Oh, sorry. My dog." She grinned at the redbone hound she'd rescued as a puppy when a group of poachers had abandoned him in the Teton wilderness. They'd been illegally using hounds—including Jack's mama—to track mountain lions, and, sensing the investigation drawing closer, had tried to cover up the crime by shooting their whole kennel and dumping the carcasses where the carrion would destroy the evidence.

The plucky pup had somehow survived a bullet wound in the hindquarters, thanks mostly to her prayers and late-night nursing, she liked to believe. Now she affectionately scratched his pink belly, laughing as he snuffled and licked her arm.

"Just one more spot on the river to check, then I promise, we can go home to a nice pasta salad and a big bowlful of Purina's finest. How does that sound?"

She laughed again as he shook his jowls at her, then snuggled deeper into the seat. "I wish all males were as easy to please as you are, you big lazy mutt."

Too bad she couldn't do the same thing, she thought, collapse on the seat without checking the last length of river. It was that darn sense of obligation again, the same trait that had made it impossible for her to put a wounded puppy to sleep.

She'd saved the best for last, though, her favorite spot of the river. She and the boys had always called this the old Standby, the place where they never failed to catch their limits.

Obviously, somebody else knew about it, she thought as she spied a muddy late-model pickup parked a few hundred yards away as she headed down the trail.

Twenty feet from the river she stopped, her hand outstretched to meet the corduroy bark of a lodgepole pine. Her attention was caught by an angler thigh-deep in the water, his line floating through the air like the silent kiss of butterfly wings.

Beauty. Simple, unadulterated beauty.

A truly skilled fly fisher could make the ordinary act of casting look as graceful and elegant as a prima ballerina pirouetting across a stage. And this one was more skilled than most, she acknowledged. With a mere flick of his wrist, he glided the line up and away from water so clear, she could see the color of each smooth stone on the bottom. She held her breath as the fly danced onto the surface, soft and easy, leaving nary a ripple to disturb the river's flow.

Carly watched, mesmerized, as a silvery flicker indicated a trout had been fooled by the deadly artificial meal, and it leaped above the water to catch it before it fluttered away. Unconsciously, she clutched the pine bark, her breath tight in her throat as, with a jerk, the fisherman set the line and the frantic trout flopped about trying to gain its freedom.

If a bee had flown in her mouth Carly wouldn't have

noticed, she was so hypnotized by the drama unraveling on the river. A more inexperienced angler would have fought the trout longer, but this expert knew the more time a fish spent on the hook the less likely it was to survive upon its release. She watched as he reeled it in quickly, mercifully, then shook his head at its diminutive size before unhooking the fly from its mouth and easing it back into the water. For a little guy, the trout had put up a heck of a fight, she thought.

The angler must have agreed with her. He tipped back his baseball cap in a silent salute, then swiped at his brow with a tanned forearm. A flash of white reflected the dying sun as he grinned, and Carly jumped as if that hypothetical bee had indeed moseyed through her fillings.

Chase. It couldn't be anybody else, not with that grin and those shoulders.

For pity's sake, how big did the territory have to be before they could stay out of each other's way? She debated turning heel and running back to the safety of her truck, but the fates again conspired against her. Just as she was about to move, he caught sight of her.

"Well, well, well. If it isn't our friendly ranger Carly!" he called, his voice echoing above the water's song.

Her lips tightened. "That's *Officer* Carly . . . uh, Officer Jacobs, thank you very much."

She walked to the river's edge. Her eyes widened and then narrowed in irritation as he waded toward her, to the shallow water near the bank. It was just like him to be wearing hip boots, instead of the more typical one-piece chest waders. He probably knew she'd always gone

a little crazy at the sight of a man wearing the former. Something about the way they hugged a man's thighs, shaping and accenting his hips and rear end, always had a strange effect on her. Sort of like the effect those half-naked musclemen on calendars had on other women.

A few feet away, still up to his calves in water, Chase cocked his head and gave a familiar, affectionate grin so potent, it nearly dissolved her antipathy—along with the support she typically relied on her knees to provide.

"You sure tracked me down in a hurry," he said, "for all your talk last night about keeping out of my way this summer. Just couldn't stay away, could you?" His grin widened and laugh lines crinkled the corners of those electric blue eyes.

The twig she didn't even know she'd been clutching snapped in two as she clenched her fist at his arrogance, teasing or not.

"Had I known you planned to fish here today, you can be sure we wouldn't be having this oh-so-delightful chat."

"But this is where I always fish," he said in a chiding tone. "You know that. It's where you cut your baby teeth on your daddy's big ol' bamboo pole."

Had she subconsciously known he would be here? Carly wondered, then quickly discarded the thought. She wasn't that weak about him. Not anymore. Was she?

That thread of uncertainty bothered her, and she spoke more harshly than she'd intended. "Show me your fishing license, Chase."

"Why certainly, Officer Jacobs," he drawled, making absolutely no move to drop his fishing rod. "As soon as you admit you knew I'd probably be here today."

She clenched her jaw. "Can the crap, Chase. I'm hot and I'm tired. This is my last stop on the Whiskey. Make it easy on both of us and break out your license so I can go home."

He shrugged. She watched impassively while he waded out of the water, set his rod down carefully on a large boulder, then patted the pockets of his khaki fishing vest.

Think of something else, Carly ordered herself, when he bent down near the rock, rear facing her, to rifle through a wicker creel resting on the shale bank. Flushed, she forced her attention to her surroundings, staring in forced fascination at a skeeter bug skating across the water.

Upstream from where they were standing, the river curled around a craggy granite cliff, only sparsely covered in brush. Where the water curved, centuries of erosion had undercut the far bank, carving out the perfect hiding place for plump fish, which would lie in wait for hatching insects to make their unsuspecting appearance.

She used to imagine that the king-sized boulders scattered throughout the riverbed had been dropped carelessly by a giant as he tromped through the mountains. They'd been perfect for basking in the summer sunshine, for watching the boys she loved wage their silly battle against Mother Nature and her scaly friends.

Later, when she was introduced to the skill and intellect involved in fishing, she'd taken over those boulders and their surrounding waters. She'd never been able to master the fine art of fly-fishing as the boys had—weak wrists, Mike used to say—but she considered herself fairly handy with a coffee can full of worms.

Carly was stunned to realize how much she would love to be stretched on one of those mighty rocks right now, rod in hand, while the water's hypnotic rhythm lulled her into a transcendental peace.

Without Chase in those damn hip waders standing entirely too near her personal comfort zone, of course.

She jerked her attention away from the flashes of the past to see Chase chewing his lip, his hands shoved into his vest pockets.

"Carly, I've, uh, got a bit of a problem."

She lifted her eyebrows. "Don't tell me. Your license is in your other pants."

"How'd you guess?"

"Because on my list of annoying phrases overused by Wyoming anglers, that ranks right up there with, 'Babe, you can bait my hook anytime.'"

He grinned and again the fading sun caught his face, reflecting silver-blue from his eyes. "Hey, babe, consider that a standing invitation, as far as I'm concerned," he teased.

Carly almost laughed with him. The temptation was so consuming she had to dig her fingernails into the palms of her hands to fight it.

Just in time, though, she remembered why she wouldn't, couldn't, share anything with Chase again, not even laughter. She set her jaw stubbornly.

"What you're telling me is you don't have a license, right?"

"Wrong. I've got a license. I, uh, just don't have it on me at this particular moment in time."

Carly's mouth stretched into a purely feline smile of anticipation. "Well then, Mr. Samuelson, I'm afraid I'm just going to have to issue you a citation. Under the laws of the state of Wyoming, statute title twenty-three, anyone who uses bait for the purpose of catching fish without the proper license issued by said state of Wyoming shall be subject to at least a hundred-dollar fine. That would be you. Sorry, pal."

"You're just loving this, aren't you?"

"No, sir." With effort, Carly straightened her features back into a serious expression. "I'm just doing my job, fulfilling my obligation to protect the wildlife of the great state of Wyoming."

"That's bull. If I were anybody else, you'd just give me a warning and go on your merry way. I think you've got some ax you'd like to grind, and you're using my butt for a whetstone."

Carly tilted her head consideringly, her attention drawn totally against her will to the way his waders outlined that particular part of his anatomy.

As the full meaning of his words sank in, though, she jerked her gaze back to his face, all thoughts of her strange attraction to him vanishing as abruptly as the fish he'd released.

"What are you accusing me of, Chase? Using my position for some personal grudge?"

"Nope," he retorted, reaching down to unhook the hip boots. "Not accusing, just stating a matter of fact."

Her angry denial clogged in her throat as he sat on a rock and started to slide his feet out of the neoprene skins, and she stumbled over the familiar intimacy of the action.

How many times had they helped each other take off a pair of waders? After a long day of standing in the uncomfortable things, it had been wonderfully luxurious to stretch her toes, especially when Chase gave her a quick foot rub to get the circulation going again.

As if he read the thought, he held up one booted foot. "Give me a hand, Carly, will you?"

Flushed by the memories, she just stared at him for a few seconds, then snapped, "No, I will not. You're a big boy, with plenty of experience taking off your own clothes, I'm sure."

Oh, Lordy. Now, what had possessed her to say something like that? Hot color soaked her face as a knowing grin played at the corners of his expressive mouth.

She ignored it, whipping out her citation book and scrawling the information needed to document the ticket. "Just sign this. You can either go to Pinedale two weeks from today to contest it or take your lumps and pay the citation."

"What happens if I don't take you up on either one of those charming options?"

"Then we arrest you," she answered smugly. "A couple of nights in jail and maybe you wouldn't be so quick to break the law next time."

"I forgot my lousy fishing license, Carly Jane. I didn't exactly knock off a liquor store."

With deceptive casualness, she bridged the few feet that separated them and slipped the citation into his vest pocket, ignoring the heat emanating from his body. She patted the pocket twice for good measure, then stepped back.

"Chase, you can rob a bank, for all I care. Or a supermarket. Or an armored truck. My jurisdiction is the

Whiskey Creek watershed, and you, my friend, are in violation of the state fishing statute. If you want to whine about it, find somebody who gives a damn."

She turned and marched back through the pines.

One eye on the door, Chase leaned back in the cheap vinyl chair in the Wind River Game and Fish district office.

"Yeah, Verl, fishing's great over on the East Fork," he continued, "if you don't mind being eaten alive by the mosquitos and the occasional game warden."

Verl Handley chuckled. "Come on, Chase, give Carly a break. She's been living with Betsy for two weeks. Knowing how edgy she's been, it's a wonder she didn't shoot first and ask questions later."

They were both chuckling when Mitch Lambert, another game warden, walked over to them.

"Verl, you'll probably want to talk to this guy on the phone."

"What's up?"

"We've got two more, up near the Fireholes."

"Damn." Verl pulled his considerable bulk out of the chair and walked to his own desk, in the corner behind a glass partition. Confused at the tense set of the other man's shoulders, Chase watched while Mitch transferred the call and Verl picked up his phone.

He was so intent on trying to figure out why the half-dozen people in the office suddenly looked so serious that he didn't see Carly enter the room. She called a greeting to Mitch, who sat at his desk listening to Verl's phone conversation.

If it hadn't hurt somewhere deep inside him, in old wounds he'd forgotten, he would have laughed at the abrupt way her warm smile froze at the mere sight of him.

"What are you doing here?" she asked rudely, throwing her coat and knapsack into the chair Verl had just vacated.

Chase forced himself to shrug nonchalantly. "Just obeying the law. Like you so sweetly told me not forty-eight hours ago, I have ten days to pay up on my citation or you'll send a warrant out for my arrest. We wouldn't want that, now would we?"

She decimated him with a glare. "I mean what are you doing here, in my chair. Get your damn boots off my desk!"

"Oh, pardon me, ma'am, is this your desk?" Ignoring the plastic nameplate clearly marking the territory as belonging to Officer Carly J. Jacobs, he raised an innocent eyebrow and dropped his feet to the floor with a thud.

"You know perfectly well it is." Her voice dropped to little more than a hiss.

He shrugged again and rose, and she immediately jumped for her seat. When he made no move to walk away, she flicked her fingers at him. "Pay your ticket with the receptionist."

Before he had a chance to reply, Verl walked the short distance from his office to Carly's desk.

"Carly, we've got a problem. A couple of hikers phoned in a report of two more grizzly carcasses up near the Firehole Lakes area, a sow and her cub. Both of them were split right down the middle, gutted and missing most of their teeth."

Chase was impressed with how swiftly Carly shifted gears. One minute she was glaring at him like a fourth grader who'd had her pigtails yanked, and the next she was an alert, composed professional. He saw just the briefest expression that looked like grief before she pulled a small spiral notebook out of the pocket of her scarlet shirt, flipped through a few pages, and began to jot notes.

"Exact location?" she asked Verl.

"Twenty miles past the trailhead, near Mitchell Springs."

"I know where it is. That's pretty rugged country."

"The worst. It'd take you two days to get in on horseback."

"Who did you say called it in?"

Verl gave the names.

"Any idea of weapon?"

"More than likely the same kind of semiautomatic, judging by their reports of the damage. The mother's head was blown clear off and her baby didn't know what hit him."

Again Chase saw Carly wince and take a quick shaky breath, but when she spoke, she showed no emotion. "Did they say how decomposed the carcasses were, so we might have some idea when it happened?"

"They were just a couple of kids. They just said it was, quote, 'pretty gross.' Does that tell you anything?"

"No, but at least they had the sense to call it in. Sounds like the same M.O., don't you think?"

"They're our guys, all right."

Chase had listened to the rapid-fire exchange in

amazement. "Whoa. Slow down. What's all this talk about M.O.s?"

"Poaching. Bears, to be exact," Verl replied. "Since the snow melted, we've found four grizzlies and twice that many black bears killed and gutted, more than likely for the gallbladders."

At his confused look, Carly spoke abruptly. "In some Asian communities, ground-up bear gallbladder is a popular folk remedy for men with, um, undependable libidos. They can be sold for upwards of eight thousand dollars each. That makes them more valuable, pound for pound, than heroin . . . and apparently somebody around here knows it."

Verl continued. "The muckety-mucks in Cheyenne sent us country boys a real professional investigator to help us get to the bottom of it." He spoke with pride. "Carly, here, is one of the best in the department for busting poaching operations. We've been lucky enough to borrow her."

In spite of himself, Chase felt his admiration grow for the little girl who used to lose her lunch at the sight of roadkill. Investigating these things couldn't be pretty, yet she'd apparently become an expert at it.

"I'll leave tomorrow morning to check it out," she said, "just as soon as I can round up some horses and my gear."

"No dice, girl." Verl shook his shaggy head. "That's a four-day trip, minimum. You know the rules. I can't let you go up there alone, and right now there's nobody else who can tag along. Thanks to these damn budget cuts, we're spread so thin I can't spare two agents until Lou comes off sick leave and Marty gets back from vacation."

"But, Verl . . ."

"Forget it, hon. It ain't happening, not unless you can rope somebody else into taking you up there . . ." His voice trailed off, and Verl looked at Chase appraisingly.

Carly caught the direction of his gaze. "No," she practically shouted, eyes wide with dawning horror. "Oh, no, you don't, Verl Handley. I'll find my own guide, or I'll wait until next week."

Chase smiled, a wide, slow smile of sheer anticipation. What goes around comes around, Officer Carly J. Jacobs, he thought.

"Come on, Carly," Verl obliged him by saying. "It's perfect. Why, Chase here knows those mountains better than just about anybody. You've got a while before the lodge gets too busy, don't you, Chase?"

As Carly turned pleading eyes to him, Chase chuckled to himself and leaned back lazily in the chair. "Sure, Verl. I can give you a few days. There's nothing I'd like better than a nice little trip up into the hills. I'd be happy to take Carly along for the ride."

She opened her mouth to protest, then shut it with a snap, her gaze dropping to the notebook in her hand. "If I wait much longer, the scavengers up there will more than likely destroy whatever evidence is left," she muttered darkly.

"Then what's the problem?"

He didn't need to be a mind reader to understand the fulminating glare she aimed in his direction. Him. That's what the problem was.

"Can you be ready by tomorrow morning?" he asked.

"Of course I can," she snapped. "The sooner we go, the sooner you can get back to leaving me alone."

He grinned. "Oh yeah, your famous blueprint for the summer. You might as well tear it up now, sweetheart. I'd say four days alone with me in the Winds is about as close as you can get to throwing a wrench into that plan."

He saw how tightly she clenched her jaw, probably to hold back an angry rejoinder. He guessed Verl's presence was inhibiting her.

With a rosy flush high on her cheek and her flashing eyes turned even darker with the irritation that filled them, she exuded passion and fire. What would she be like in his arms with all that energy channeled into an entirely different direction? he wondered, then cursed silently for conjuring up that image as he felt himself growing aroused.

He cleared his throat. "I've got to run a few errands while I'm in town, but why don't we talk about what supplies you want me to provide over lunch at RJ's? My treat."

"Sure, next time there's a blizzard in hell."

"I was thinking more along the lines of an hour or so," he replied blandly. "I'll stop by here when I've finished and we can walk over together."

She muttered an extremely unladylike order and Chase grinned. "Carly Jane!" he admonished. "Now what would your mother say if she heard talk like that? Knowing Betsy, I'm sure she taught you to use a much more gracious manner when accepting a luncheon invitation."

In a silky-smooth voice that would have drawn flies,

she repeated the request. Chase laughed and walked toward the door. "See you in an hour. Don't bother dressing up!"

Despite her unabated annoyance, Carly couldn't help but be thrust back to a different lifetime when she and Chase walked into RJ's Café. As soon as Chase extended his arm—a firmly muscled arm that she pinched herself for noticing—to open the aging wooden door, all heads in the joint swiveled in their direction to survey the new-comers.

She spared a quick look around while Chase greeted several people she vaguely recognized. Other than some cheap brass-framed wildlife prints on the walls and a few more water spots on the ceiling, the place hadn't changed.

At least six different kinds of paneling—all of them unattractive—covered the walls in a haphazard decorating job. The same cracked red vinyl stools surrounded the bar, its gray-speckled finish worn thin in places by more than thirty years of elbows. The sound of grease spattering and billiard balls bouncing off each other competed with the comfortable din of laughter and chatter in the old place, and a haze of old cigarette smoke lent a surrealistic edge to the scene.

Despite its homely appearance, RJ's was the hub for socializing in this corner of the county. The food was hot and plentiful, and old-timers could always find somebody they knew to exchange a few laughs with.

A deep sense of loss settled low in her stomach as she watched Chase stop at a booth where an older couple sat. He slapped the man on the back and kissed the woman's cheek, and Carly had to swallow against emotion at the warm, down-home friendliness of the place. Lord she'd missed this! It was like being shown an amputated limb she hadn't even known was gone.

"Carly, come on over here," Chase ordered. He flashed her a one-sided grin that, despite her firm resolve, had the same effect on her as a caress. "You remember Marge and Leon Simmons?"

Of course she did. Marge used to teach Sunday school, and she often warned Carly she was headed for "big trouble" if she didn't learn to sit still for longer than two minutes. Apparently the dire prophesy had been forgotten. Before she could say a word, the older woman pulled Carly down into a tight embrace, pressing a warm, weathered cheek to hers. Just as abruptly, Marge thrust her away.

"Carly Jacobs, let me get a good look at you." Carly flushed as intense green eyes scanned her features. "Why, honey, you've gone and grown up into a downright beautiful girl. Didn't she?" Marge glared at her husband of forty-seven years, as if daring him to contradict her.

"She surely did," Leon dutifully replied.

"Chase, what do you think?" Marge demanded.

He tilted his head and pretended to assess her. "Sexy as hell," he said gruffly, loud enough for only her to hear. Warmth sizzled through her like hot oil on a griddle, and she had to grip the table edge for support. They stared at each other for a moment, oblivious to the clatter around them, to the jukebox blaring a honky-tonk tune about lonesome nights and cheatin' hearts, until Marge broke the spell.

"Speak up, boy. What'd you say?"

Chase turned back to the couple, a distracted frown lining his forehead. "I said she's real pretty," he replied.

After a few minutes of chitchat, he ushered her to a nearby booth and slid onto the vinyl seat across from her.

What exactly just happened? Carly wondered, dazed. Her skin seemed oddly tight, as if she'd just stepped out of a hot bath, and she felt weak and jittery from being impaled by the full force of his glittering eyes. This was Chase, she reminded herself. The one she was supposed to despise.

His voice, smooth and unruffled, broke into her internal lecture. "I'm sure you'll be pleased to know RJ has gone cosmopolitan since you've been away. Monday's lunch special is a little taste of Paris, with either French dip sandwiches or hearty French onion soup. Both, of course, served with french-fried potatoes, not your everyday home fries, mind you."

How could he talk about food when the world had just shifted on its axis? she wondered.

"Do you think they'd kick me out if I just ordered a salad?" she managed to ask.

He winked at her. "Not if you pour a ton of French dressing on it. Bud-ump-bump."

Carly laughed, a short laugh that she bit off abruptly. She'd done it, she thought. She'd actually laughed at a joke made by Chase Samuelson. And not a very good one at that. A wild, desperate urge to flee filled her. She wanted to escape to the café's sorry excuse for a ladies room and see whether she'd find her own face staring back at her from the dingy mirror, or whether some alien life form with a particular fondness for blue eyes and to-die-for shoulders had invaded her body when she wasn't looking.

Though really, it hadn't killed her to relax a little around him, she mused. For at least the next four days they'd be in each other's company constantly. If she spent the entire time prickling whenever he so much as blinked at her, she'd be more strung out than if she had to spend the whole summer living with her mother.

Determined to ease off on the antagonism, she offered a weak half smile. He looked startled, but then returned her attempt by showing off those blasted deep dimples of his. Ridiculous, she thought in irritation, that he could look so utterly male with dimples. Girls in flouncy dresses should have dimples. Chubby bald babies, maybe. Not a retired professional athlete who ran a wilderness guide service, and who practically oozed potent masculinity.

She realized she was staring when he cleared his throat, a sheepish expression in his eyes and a flush sneaking across his cheekbones. Well, she thought, fancy that. Chase Samuelson was embarrassed about his dimples. Who'd have believed it?

He cleared his throat again. "I had a few minutes while one of my horses was being shod over at the blacksmith's, so I made a list of supplies we'll need." He slid a piece of paper across the table, and Carly gave it a cursory examination. "We don't do too many guided trips anymore, but when we do, the Lazy Jake generally provides just about everything—food, water, tents, that sort of thing. You're welcome to bring anything you feel you need that's not on the list, provided you don't pack more than about seventy-five pounds. No barbells or anything."

"What about taking along a lazy redbone hound?"

"That's fine, as long as he doesn't need an extra horse."

She'd done it again. He'd managed to elicit a genuine, spontaneous smile from her. Easy, girl, she thought. Next thing you know, you'll be one of those brainless women who probably flutter their eyelashes at him and giggle at every utterance coming out of that beautiful mouth.

She forced her attention back to the conversation. "Jack is perfectly capable of walking, when he puts his mind to it."

"Jack?"

"My dog. Jackson. I'd leave him with my mother, but besides her claims to be terrified of him, he's fairly handy to have along on an investigation. The hound in him can scent out all kinds of clues."

"What kind of information are we going to be looking for?"

She sniffed. "*We* aren't going to be looking for anything. Your job is to get me there and back, not to act out any lingering childhood Hardy boys fantasies you might have."

"Aw, Carly," he complained, and she watched in fascination as only his left dimple appeared when he offered a lopsided grin. "I guess that means I'm stuck with my grown-up fantasies then, right?"

A shiver skipped through her as that strange glint

reappeared in his eyes. Holy Moses, the man was lethal. Summoning her self-control, she managed a smirk.

"Fine, Chase. Just keep me out of them."

"Too late," she thought she heard him mutter, but a dropped glass shattered behind the bar and she couldn't be sure.

THREE

"Mother? Have you seen a box marked Camping Stuff?" Carly tried to outshout the canned laughter coming from the television in the living room down the hall from her childhood room, now filled ceiling-high with brown cardboard boxes she hadn't yet taken to the cabin.

"Don't you raise your voice at me, Carly Jane. I can hear you just fine without you yelling like you're calling pigs to the trough." Betsy Jacobs, petite and graceful, without so much as a smudge to mar her immaculately groomed person, appeared in the doorway. "No, I haven't seen it, although to be truthful, I haven't dared come in here for fear something will topple over on me. Heaven knows what you have in all these boxes." She gave a delicate shudder that barely rippled her sugar-white sweater.

Just for the sake of contrast, Carly took a look at herself in the mirror over the cream-colored Provincial–French style vanity that matched the rest of the frilly bedroom set thrust upon her as a preteen. In a hurry to gather her gear she'd thrown on her oldest sweats—the ones where the elastic in the waist had long since lost its grab—and had hurriedly caught her hair in back with the rubber band from the day's newspaper. She looked like either a Salvation Army reject or a waifishly hip teenager.

Sighing, she turned back to Betsy. "Well, Mother, one box is filled with camping supplies, things I'll be needing in less than twelve hours. Unfortunately, it's the one I can't seem to find."

"Did you try your closet?"

Carly snapped her fingers and dived for it, shoving aside her ski boots and a pile of old magazines to slide open the door. "Bingo!" she yelled from inside the closet. With a mighty heave, she jerked it out from under a box labeled Ugly Sweaters and another marked Textbooks I'll Probably Never Use Again.

She managed somehow to pull the unwieldy box out of the closet, then she plopped on the floor to sort through what she needed.

"You know, dear," Betsy said, "as much as I wish you didn't have to go up in the mountains with the weather so uncertain, I'm glad you at least have the good sense to take Chase along with you. He's a good boy and he'll see that you stay safe and warm."

Genuinely surprised, both at her mother's words and that she was still in the room, Carly glanced up from pawing through the box. Her mother was clearing a spot on the bed before settling her trim bottom on the flowered bedspread.

"What do you mean he's a good boy?" Carly asked warily.

"Just what I said," Betsy answered, her mouth drawn into a prim line. "So many of the young people in your generation only worry about silly things like spotted owls and IRAs. They don't have time to see that an old woman has enough firewood to get her through the winter or to battle six-foot snowdrifts to shovel her sidewalks and bring her groceries."

Chase did that? Carly's hands stilled their search through the box. The idea of him being so concerned about her mother sent a warmth washing through her, but even as she felt a half smile take over her mouth, she forced a grimace. Knowing Chase Samuelson, he probably had an ulterior motive. For the life of her, she couldn't figure out what it could be right at this moment, but give her time. She had loads of experience assigning ulterior motives to his every action.

"That's right," her mother continued, "and I'm not the only one. He also took the time to shovel Mrs. Hardaway's driveway and that nice Mr. Gomez's down the street. You know, he's got that arthritis that makes it so hard for him to get along."

"Lucky for Chase," Carly said waspishly, "he can afford to be generous with his time. If I had the salary he earned just from his five seasons in the majors I could spend my leisure time taking care of the whole town. Besides," she added more gently, "you're not an old woman. You happen to be a very young-looking fifty-eight, Mother, not quite ready for support hose and liver-spot remover."

Betsy shook her head, her expression plainly conveying her habitual disappointment in her only daughter. Seeing it, Carly felt a not uncommon urge to throw something. Not necessarily at Betsy, but perhaps in that general direction. . . .

She adored her mother. She really did! It was just hard to remember that sometimes when they were within, oh, say, the same time zone. Oil and vinegar, that's what they were. Two women who had little in common except cocoa eyes and the two men they'd both loved. Carly had never been the daughter Betsy wanted and Betsy couldn't understand the woman her daughter had become. Carly knew both of them recognized their failures and were saddened by it.

"Carly Jane? Did you hear me?"

She shook her thoughts away. "Sorry, Mother. What did you say?"

"I said, I've always thought Chase would make some lucky girl a wonderful husband. He's so considerate and has such a darling way with children. Whenever he comes out to church—not as often as I'd like, mind you, but often enough—he sits with his sister Penny and helps her with those twins. Oh, what a handful they are! But Chase manages to take their shenanigans in stride."

Carly tightened her hands on a bandanna in the box, wrapping it around her fingers while she tried to ignore the effusive praise.

"And he's so handsome, too," Betsy went on, "with those eyes and those dimples. One hunky babe. Isn't that what they call them these days?"

She couldn't stand it. Not one more word. Especially not when her mother's praise so accurately described her own confusing thoughts toward the man. "What Chase Samuelson is, Mother," she blurted out, "is a no-good, lying bastard who wouldn't think twice about stabbing his best friend in the back."

Betsy gasped and narrowed her eyes at her daughter. "Carly Jane Jacobs, I refuse to have talk like that in my house."

"Talk like what?" she asked quietly, keeping her gaze averted and her hands busy picking through the camping supplies. "Like the 'good boy' who brings your groceries and shovels your snow is also the 'good boy' who happens to have killed your son?" She looked up. "Or have you forgotten Mike? It's been ten years, after all, since Chase made him drive his truck off a mountain. Memories probably tend to blur with all those good works going around."

As soon as the nasty words were out, hanging in the air like a stale smog, Carly wholeheartedly wished she could recall them. Before her eyes, Betsy withered, finally looking all of her fifty-eight years. She sat back, one hand fluttering at her lips, her eyes stark and forlorn—the eyes of a woman who mourned the loss of both a husband and a child.

"Oh, Mother, I'm sorry." Swearing at her own insensitivity, Carly climbed on the bed and clutched Betsy's smooth, cool hand between her own. Betsy always seemed so tranquil, even when she was up to her carefully plucked eyebrows commanding this charity or that cause. Seeing her calm facade shatter into pieces jolted Carly more than she cared to admit. "I'm so sorry," she repeated. "I didn't mean that. I know you miss Mikey as much as I do . . ."

"More."

Carly could barely hear the low-pitched word, but

the intensity behind it brought a vicious stinging to her eyes. She squeezed her mother's hand and, for a few minutes, the two of them sat in silence on the bed, their thoughts filled with the laughing boy they'd both loved so dearly.

"But Mom," Carly said finally, "Chase isn't Mikey."

"I know that, dear. I also know that, no matter what you say, he was always a good boy and he's grown into a very thoughtful, very admirable man."

"If you say so." Sliding her hand away, Carly returned to the floor. The virtues of Chase Samuelson, or the lack thereof, weren't something she felt capable of debating.

"I do say so," Betsy said, her features once again placid and serene. She stood, brushing at nonexistent wrinkles in her pants. "I just never could understand this ridiculous belief of yours that Chase was to blame for Mike's death. How could Chase have caused it from Arizona, at that baseball practice thing they make those poor ballplayers do every year?"

"Spring training," Carly corrected her automatically.

"What's that?"

"It's called spring training. Chase was in Phoenix for spring training when Mike died."

"There, you see? He couldn't have caused Mike's death from seven hundred miles away, now could he? Mike went into a coma because he tried to forget he was a diabetic, refusing to follow his diet or inject his insulin, things he'd been doing all his life. It was just plain stupid. He went into severe insulin shock and that's what caused his accident, you know that as well as I do. It certainly wasn't Chase's fault."

Carly clamped her lips to hold back the denials crowding in her throat. Her mother had refused to see the hell that Mike had been living in, had ignored the way he'd changed. Carly knew what Chase's betrayal had done to her brother, how he had virtually stopped living after his best friend had left town with Mike's fiancée.

The spring Mike died, Chase had been in his rookie season, so enthralled by his new life as a professional athlete that he hadn't even spared a weekend to return to Whiskey Creek for his best friend's funeral. Neither had Mike's girlfriend of four years, Jessie Palmer, the woman he'd planned to marry. The little bitch who'd wasted no time hitching her wagon to Chase's star, probably hoping for the money and fame of life in the big leagues.

Neither one of them had cared what their playing house together had done to Mike or about the dark rumors of pregnancy that had followed them to California.

Carly had been seventeen that miserable spring. Seventeen. The age when most girls were going to high school dances and flirting with all the neighborhood boys. Instead, she'd been devastated by her brother's death and, in secret, mourning the loss of her silly childish dreams about Chase.

From the time she was old enough to understand the concept, she had sworn to anyone who would listen that someday, somehow, somewhere, she and Chase Samuelson would marry. When she turned nine, she started telling him several times a week that he was her boyfriend, just to warn him so he wouldn't waste his time with any of the grown-up girls who watched him with admiring eyes. He would always laugh indulgently at her bossy tone, kiss her obligingly on the cheek, and tell her that the day she could beat him at arm wrestling would be the day he'd meet her at the altar.

Mike's death had changed all that.

Carly realized now that that spring had been one of those defining moments that philosophers talk about, a season that forever changed how she confronted the world. Before that, she had been innocent and eager to meet life head on. She'd had faith in two things: her family loved her and the Wyoming sun rose and set according to the demands of Chase Samuelson.

His betrayal and its horrifying impact on all their lives had shaken her to the core. More than that, it had changed her, hardened her, in ways even she didn't totally understand.

A decade later, she liked to think her hurts had scarred over, until she was tough enough to handle anything. Yet even with the new strength, parts of her that Chase had wounded would never be the same.

She wrenched her thoughts from the past and returned her attention to Betsy. "Let's drop the subject of Chase for now, please."

Her mother smiled. "Fine, dear. I've got to take my oatmeal crunchies out of the oven anyway. I made them for you to take tomorrow. They were always Chase's favorite, don't you remember? How would you like one right now, with a big glass of milk?"

Stifling a groan, Carly smiled weakly at the eager pampering. "Sure, Mother, that would be fine."

It would probably be like chewing wallpaper paste, considering the butterflies that were suddenly swarming around her stomach at the reminder of her upcoming ordeal. But she'd already reached her daily quota of hurting her mother's feelings.

After Betsy returned to the kitchen, Carly rested her head against the wall, mindless of the sprigs of pink flowers in little baskets that dotted the paper against her cheek.

She closed her eyes wearily. How in the world was she going to survive four days alone with him? Besides the baffling attraction that terrified her psyche as much as it aroused her body, they practically needed an extra horse just to pack all the emotional baggage between them.

Four days. Ninety-six hours. Roughly six thousand minutes alone with those damn dimples.

God help her.

Dawn showed only as a pink rim along the mountains the next morning when Chase stopped his pickup in front of the Jacobses' cabin, a quad horse trailer in tow behind him.

This was, without question, his favorite time of day, he decided, as he turned the truck off and sat for a few minutes, absorbing the hush of the early morning darkness. The day hadn't had a chance to make an appearance yet. It hovered just over the mountains, a possibility waiting to explode on the horizon.

He found an almost guilty pleasure in enjoying this predawn peacefulness while most of the world slumbered on, in sorting through his thoughts with a mind clear and unburdened.

Something about the anticipation zinging through

him reminded him of long-ago fishing trips, when Jake would pull him out of bed and the two of them would sneak out of the house, trying to gather their gear as quietly as possible so they wouldn't awaken his grandmother and sisters.

They'd load up Jake's battered old '59 Chevy pickup with their tackle and a cooler filled with lunch. He'd doze in the corner of the seat while Jake headed for this very cabin, where Mike and Carly would usually be waiting for them on the front porch.

Chase smiled, bittersweet. The days when she would greet him with a sleepy hug and a big, wet kiss on the cheek were long gone, probably never to return.

A dog's lazy bark jolted him from the past. He climbed out of the truck to see the door to the cabin open and Carly silhouetted by the soft light glowing from inside.

"Mornin'," he called, tucking his shirt in as he headed up the walk.

She raised a hand in greeting and stood leaning against the doorframe, the mug of coffee in her hand sending spirals of steam into the crisp, sweet mountain air. For one tiny instant of male vanity, Chase was inordinately grateful that his bum knees were fresh and rested. At least he didn't have to hobble up the steps while she scrutinized him. The left leg had a little hitch in it, but if he walked slowly enough, she wouldn't be able to tell. The woman obviously already despised him—no sense giving her that weakness to chew on, as well.

"I'm almost ready," she said, when he reached the

top step and stood on the wide planks of the cabin's front porch. "I just need to grab my gear."

He shrugged. "We've got time."

Before he could say anything else, she disappeared inside. He followed, watching her enter a back room that he knew had belonged to her parents when they spent the summers up here.

He strolled into the main room of the cabin that served as living room, dining room, and kitchen. It was a small dwelling, not much bigger than the gathering room at the Lazy Jake, but the size lent itself to coziness, not claustrophobia. Already Carly had managed to inject some of her personality into the home: a stack of paperbacks here, a collection of fossils there, a bright splash of color from a crimson-and-blue Navajo blanket draped over the back of the plump old couch.

Gracing the wall opposite the wide stone fireplace was a massive print of a gray wolf, its head cocked, its red eyes watchful as a wolf cub frolicked underfoot. He immediately recognized the work of Keenan Malone, the premier wildlife photographer in the West. For the first time since she'd returned to town, he felt a strong sense of kinship with her. He had two Malones hanging in his bedroom.

He started to walk over for a closer look, but a collection of scrapbooks cluttering the top of a scarred pine bureau distracted him. Several of them lay open, as if they'd been looked at recently, and curiosity teased him.

He changed directions to go look at them, and was confronted by the whole Jacobs clan in various stages of growth. On one of the open pages, he saw Carly as a curly headed toddler, clutching a daisy and beaming angelically at the camera. The Hummelian perfection of the scene was marred only by a big purple stain on her cheek—grape jelly, he assumed—and the enormous spider in her other hand, which she looked ready to pop into her mouth.

He flipped through a few more pages, then paused when another image leaped out at him—a fifteen-year-old Mike and a skinny eleven-year-old Carly in swimming suits, with two inner tubes propped on the ground nearby. Both grinned cheekily, flexing their biceps, fists in the air, like bodybuilders posing in competition.

Quintessential Mike, he thought, smiling himself. Full of life, fast talking, and eager to take on any challenge. He'd been a natural leader, whether it was plotting tricks against their long-suffering elementary school teachers or coaxing Chase into risky adventures. From the day he and Chase gave each other fat lips and tough reputations with their first and only fight—in third grade, over a pig-tailed flirt named Anabel Jenkins—Mike had taken the shy, confused, lonely boy Chase had been under his considerable wing.

Mike had taught him how to swear eloquently and babysat him through fractions; Chase, in turn, had introduced his friend to fishing and the fine art of ditching Sunday school. They'd gone on their first sweaty-palmed date together, had nursed each other through their first hangover, and spent countless nights trading dreams under the stars.

Lord, he missed him. Chase touched his thumb to the face grinning at him from the picture, a familiar ache low in his gut. Mike had been dead for ten years, but he still felt the loss as acutely as he had the day he learned of Mike's death.

And Carly. What a ham she'd been, always trying to keep up with two rowdy older boys. Funny how most of the time he and Mike hadn't minded her tagging along. Maybe it was because they got such a kick out of her spunky attempts to emulate everything they did, whether it was a moonlight game of kick the can in the wooded foothills between their cabins or riding the rapids in skimpy inner tubes.

Mike had plainly adored his only sister, despite their age difference. At first, Chase had teased him about having to take a little kid wherever he went, but Mike never complained about having her along. After a while, Chase didn't either. They both knew that if they didn't let her trail after them, she'd follow them anyway, and Mike would get in trouble because he hadn't watched out for his little sister.

A sound near the doorway distracted him, and he looked up to see the woman that plucky little girl had grown into walking out of the back room with a bedroll and a duffel bag.

She stopped a few feet away, a canteen hanging from her shoulder like other women would carry a purse, a camera slung around her neck. It was his first clear look at her since he'd arrived, and he had to take a shaky breath and carefully set down the scrapbook, fiercely trying not to gawk.

She was wearing an old pair of blue jeans, faded nearly white, and an oversized burgundy flannel shirt, flaps untucked, that swamped her slim figure. Instead of disguising her delicate curves, though, it just made her legs look long and unbearably sexy in the form-fitting jeans, firing his imagination into overdrive.

He figured she must have pulled her hair back into a braid when it was still wet. It hung long and heavy down her back and a few damp tendrils had escaped. They framed a face Chase decided he could stare at all day. Those warm chocolate eyes, challenging and uncertain at the same time, dominated her features. But his gaze was inexorably drawn to her lips, full and ripe and sweet. A grimace thinned them into a tight line, but the stern expression did nothing to hide their lush appeal.

Tucked into the corner of her mouth was a white dab of toothpaste, and Chase had to curl his hands into fists against the powerful urge to cross the room and flick his tongue in that very spot before devouring her mouth with his own. She must have caught the direction of his gaze—he passionately hoped she couldn't detect the hunger too—because her own tongue darted out and searched for the wayward speck.

Instantly, blood pooled in his groin at the unconsciously provocative gesture. In his mind flashed a vision of him cupping her face in his hands and lowering his head slowly until their lips barely touched, her cool breath against his mouth, welcoming, tantalizing. He closed his eyes, the image so vivid that he could almost taste her, almost feel the slick texture of mouth on mouth, tongue against tongue, as she opened for him, as she melted into him.

"Is it gone?" she asked tersely.

"Wha-at?" Chase stammered, eyes blinking open. For a panicked second, he thought she'd seen into his mind, into his entirely too active imagination.

"Whatever you were staring at. Did I get it?"

Unfortunately for the sake of his willpower, no. Spending four days together, he suddenly realized, might be annoying for her, but it would be sheer torture for him. Especially given the antagonism she made no effort to hide, the waves of anger that radiated around her like the silken strands of a spider web.

"Yeah," he lied, uncomfortably aroused and confused that she could so easily bring him to such a state just by glaring at him. "Yeah, it's gone."

"Great." She shifted her grip on the duffel bag, and he immediately moved forward to help her with the bulky load, only to be met by a scowl. "I can carry my own gear."

"Fine," he snapped. He abruptly turned and walked back outside to the truck, smoldering while she hefted her gear into the bed, then whistled for a lean, red, jowly hound that looked like he outweighed her. The dog lumbered into the bed of the pickup, and she watched to make sure he was settled before climbing into the cab.

Still annoyed, Chase started the truck and pulled back onto the dirt road that would lead them to the trailhead. From there, they had two days worth of pounding high mountain trails to find the spot where the bears had been killed.

They traveled in silence for a few minutes, the throb of the engine and the humming of the tires on the still-wet road the only sounds to disturb the awkwardness between them.

He couldn't get a break with her if he jumped out of an airplane without a parachute, Chase thought. Even when he tried to be courteous, just as he would with any other member of the human race, she acted like he'd goosed her or something. *Give it up, buddy*, an irate little voice in his head commanded. *There's no way you're going to break through the barrier she's erected between you two.*

Carly Jacobs would hang on to her convictions—her belief that he had caused Mike's death—like a grizzly bear guarding her cubs.

He sighed, not realizing he'd made the sound out loud until she spoke.

"Chase, I'm sorry," she said quietly.

He glanced at her, cautious and hopeful at the same time. "For . . . ?"

"Snapping at you back there when you tried to help me. Under the best of circumstances, I'm cranky first thing in the morning. This is obviously not the best of circumstances."

Her words hovered in the air between them, and his shoulders slumped. Not exactly the most heartfelt of apologies, he thought. And not what he wanted to hear her apologize for, either.

"Anyway," she went on, "I'm grumpier than normal today. I spent most of last night looking through boxes for supplies and—"

"Forget it," he said, disappointment sharpening his tone more than he'd intended.

Silence descended on the cab again. He tapped his fingers on the wheel, then, in desperation, turned on the radio. Carly jumped as static blared into the tense quiet.

"Sorry," he muttered, adjusting the dial in vain. They must be too sheltered by the surrounding mountains for any kind of reception, he figured. His left hand on the wheel, he reached across the seat to search the jockey box for a tape to play. The position brought his forearm across her knees, and even through the denim he could feel the warmth of her, burning like a forest fire scorching a stand of pines.

He had only the briefest of moments to relish the contact before she flinched and drew backward in the seat.

"Sorry," he said automatically, fumbling for the latch on the box. It hurt him, this bristly attitude she'd adopted toward him, filling him with a deep sense of loss.

The day he found out about Mike's death, two days after the funeral, when his grandmother finally tracked him down at the hospital where Jessie was struggling to keep her baby, he had called to comfort Carly. A grieving and apologetic Betsy told him she refused to talk to him. At the time he'd assumed she was too overwhelmed to share her sorrow with him.

When he finally had a chance to return to Whiskey Creek during the all-star break in July, she studiously avoided him. She'd hang up the phone when she heard his voice and conveniently disappear whenever he tried to confront her.

He should have explained everything to her, he acknowledged now, despite the pain he knew it would have caused. But he'd been so young, barely twenty-one, and he'd been stunned by the awful pain of Mike's death and his own frantic struggle to survive his rookie season when all he had wanted to do was crawl back to the security of home.

And then there'd been Jessie. In her way, she'd needed him more than Carly. Carly at least had had her parents to help pull her through the pain, but Jessie had been forced to depend on only him. He'd been a self-absorbed young man back then, insecure and immature—he would be the first to admit it. But he'd done one thing right in his life by taking Jessie with him, and he couldn't regret it. Not even to appease the woman sitting next to him.

Hell, he thought, the only way to appease Carly would be to open the truck door and take a flying leap into the sagebrush. The idea of him, bad knees and all, diving from a moving vehicle because of a wisp of a woman made him chuckle and almost forget he was still leaning half over her, his hand deep inside the jockey box.

"Do you mind?" she said, inching even farther away.

"Sorry," he said, for the umpteenth time, and grabbed the first tape his fingers encountered. He popped it into the truck's cassette player, and Emmylou Harris's voice filled the cab.

His choice of music, or perhaps it was just his movement back to the other side of the truck, was rewarded by a smile. Carly leaned back against the seat, eyes closed while the familiar song surrounded them, filling the emptiness between them with sweet, lilting beauty.

She mouthed a few of the lyrics, and Chase had to smother a grin when her jaw stretched into a wide yawn, halfway through the chorus.

"We've still got nearly an hour before we reach the trailhead," he said. "Why don't you try to get some sleep?" Even before he finished the question, she was settling back in the seat, as cozy as a baby lamb nestling into warm hay.

She must have intercepted his amused look because she glared at him through half-closed eyes. "I can't sleep," she muttered. "You're the worst driver in Sublette County. Everybody knows that. You go way too fast, and I swear, you must have a map of every blasted pothole in the road, and a few more besides. I have to stay awake so I can push us out when we get high-centered . . ." Her voice trailed off, and she drifted into sleep, lulled by the music and the motion of the truck.

Still the same Carly, he thought, chuckling softly. She'd been making fun of his driving abilities since he ripped out the mayor's fence during his driver's test.

She also used to be able to sleep anywhere, he remembered. Curled up on a tree stump. On a rocky beach with a fishing rod in her hand. Even on horseback. He and Mike used to place bets about it, coming up with outlandish locales for her naps, then putting her in the situations to see whether she could pull it off.

He tilted his head to look at her, drinking in the sight of long lashes fanning high cheekbones and her freshly scrubbed skin. Her lower lip jutted into a pout as she slept, and he gripped the steering wheel hard, stung by a sudden, almost violent urge to suckle there.

In the flint-gray light of early morning she looked impossibly alluring, sexy and innocent at the same time. Within reach of his fingers, yet as far away emotionally as she'd been for the last decade.

No, he corrected his earlier thoughts. She wasn't the same little girl. Not anymore. This Carly Jacobs was a woman he knew only minimally and understood even less. Give him time, though. By the end of this trip, he was going to break through those barriers if he had to use a sledgehammer to do it.

He risked another look at her, smiling at her child-like pose. An elbow rested on the window frame and she slept with her cheek propped against a fist, the other hand curled in her lap. She murmured a mewling little sound, and Chase finally gave in to his body's demand for contact. He covered her hand with his own, then drew it to his lips to press a barely-there kiss on a knuckle.

"Welcome home, Carly," he whispered.

FOUR

"Hey, sunshine, wake up. This is your stop."

Carly heard the voice just beyond her consciousness, on the other side of the soft haze that surrounded her. She tried to shut it out, only vaguely aware that the rocking motion of the last twenty miles had ceased.

Through the thick layers of sleep, she felt something warm and hard brush her cheek and instinctively she rubbed against it, smelling soap and leather. Chase. Even in her dreams, she couldn't escape him.

The heaven of it was, she'd learned years ago that this was the one place she didn't have to try.

Through their years of separation, when thoughts of him were etched with acid pain and bone-deep loneliness, only in her sleep could she remember the Chase she had loved. Only here, amid the tangled threads of the memories she suppressed during the day, could she relive cheering for him at a high school baseball game or begging him for rides on the motorcycle he'd proudly purchased with hard-won savings the summer of his senior year.

Only here could she once again sit on one of the old rocking chairs on the Lazy Jake's screened back porch and play cards with Chase and Mike while a summer thunderstorm washed the heat away, or tag along while the boys moved irrigation pipe in the far pastures.

The dreams had faded since she'd become an adult, but once or twice a year they would return, vivid and real and piercing in their intensity.

A few months ago, she'd watched a televised baseball game with some friends in Cheyenne, and the announcer had mentioned Chase's name in connection with some obscure statistic. That night, he'd come to her in her sleep, uttering husky apologies and holding her face pressed to his solid chest while she cried away the years of confused misery.

She'd awakened with damp cheeks, a pillow crushed in her arms, and a hollow ache deep inside.

This wasn't the same, though. In this dream Chase carried no apologies, just heat and hard strength. She smiled at the chimera and turned her head to slide her lips to his wrist, set free by the knowledge that in the refuge of sleep, she could lower her guard.

She heard him mutter what sounded like a cross between a prayer and a curse, she couldn't tell which. It was *her* dream, after all, and if she didn't want to bother figuring it out, nobody could make her. So there. She giggled at her childish thoughts, then abruptly stopped when she felt a different kind of touch, warm lips at the corner of her mouth, hard hands cupping her face. Ahhh.

This had never happened in one of her dreams before, had it? It felt so incredibly right that she wondered why it hadn't. Then the kiss deepened, and she forgot about the puzzle and gave herself up to the pleasure of his touch.

Her dream lover kissed as she'd always imagined the real man would kiss, gently at first, soft as the down from the cottonwoods behind the cabin, then pressing deeper, demanding more from her. His tongue tickled her lips, and she willingly opened for him, exulting in the taste of him.

He feels so real, she thought, awed by the power of her own imagination. So real and so completely perfect. He drew back then, as if to snatch his warmth away, and she murmured his name in protest, flinging her arms around his neck and holding tight in an effort to stretch out the vivid dream.

It was the swearing that finally dragged her from sleep.

"Carly, honey, Lord knows I don't want to stop. But you'll hate me even more if I don't. Wake up, dammit."

Her eyelids jerked open, and, horrified, she stared at electric blue eyes mere centimeters from her own. Consciousness crashed in and she froze, his head still cradled tightly in her arms, then she scrambled away, bumping into the passenger door of the pickup so hard, the door handle gouged into her back.

Rapid breathing filled the interior of the truck, and she shuddered to realize it came from both of them.

"I . . . You . . . What was that . . . ?" Her voice trailed off. As much as she wanted to rail at him for touching her, for daring to ignore the blunt distaste she'd tried to convey around him, she knew who held most of the blame for the kiss. It didn't matter that she'd been half-asleep. With cruel clarity, she remembered her lips pressed to his wrist, felt again the whisper of coarse dark hair against her mouth and her hands clenched around his neck.

Carly wanted to run, as far and as fast as she could, from the knowledge that a large part of her still objected strenuously to the loss of his closeness.

"Carly." He spoke her name softly, and stark desire stared at her from across the width of the truck, his eyes smoky with need.

"You . . . We shouldn't have . . . Please don't touch me again," she practically begged, fumbling behind her for the door handle. With an urgency born of desperation, she scurried out of the truck and back to the bed, where Jackson waited patiently. He barked at her approach and leaped over the side, wagging his tail and sniffing her hands as if he hadn't seen her in months.

Carly grabbed him and buried her face in his short, bristly hide, trying to still the quaking in her insides.

She had never, in all her twenty-seven years, reacted to a man so physically. Even now, despite her shame and confusion, she could feel the need pulsing through her. A man without morals could have stripped her naked and taken her, and she wouldn't have been able to bring herself to protest. She frowned at the thought. Hadn't she decided a decade ago that Chase was just such a man, without morals, without a glimmer of decency?

The driver's side door slammed hard, and a few seconds later she could feel Chase towering behind her.

The hairs on the back of her neck prickled and she tensed, waiting.

"Run all you want, little girl," Chase said huskily, his cowboy drawl more pronounced than usual. "Sooner or later, you're not gonna move fast enough, and I'll be right there waitin' to catch you."

With that, he started unloading their gear from the truck as if the passion of a few minutes before had been nothing more than a casual good-morning kiss between longtime lovers.

Carly didn't know whether to be upset at his ease in shaking off the heat they generated, or relieved that he didn't pursue it. She was relieved, she finally told herself firmly. Relieved and grateful that he didn't ask why a woman who supposedly hated him had whispered his name in passion. She sighed and rested her cheek on the dog's back as she watched Chase work.

He moved effortlessly, fluidly, with economical movements and impressive strength. He used one hand to pick up two cast-iron dutch ovens that had to weigh fifteen pounds each, acting as if they were empty shopping bags, and Carly grimaced.

The rust chamois shirt he wore stretched and pulled as he reached into the truck, the soft fabric giving her an all-too-clear idea of the muscles that lay beneath it. He was rough and male, from the faded jeans encasing powerful thighs to the leather gloves he casually shoved into his back pocket, to that *Marlboro Man* mustache.

She sighed again. Why couldn't he have some obvious imperfection, like squinty eyes or big ears or a beer belly? Oh, no, not Chase Samuelson. When God decided to create the perfect man, he did it with a vengeance, giving him everything a woman could possibly find desirable. Long eyelashes. Handsome, rugged features. An athlete's body chock-full of thick muscle and lean grace. And those eyes, eyes that could sizzle with energy or turn languid and fathomless, giving a woman ideas she had no business thinking.

Naturally, the Big Guy then had to go and plop him right here in the middle of Wyoming to make Carly's life—or the next few days of it, at least—one heck of a lesson in self-control.

Just then he turned his head and for a few seconds stood there, head cocked, his eyes locked with hers. A blush spread from the roots of her hair to her neck. He obviously knew she'd been watching him, but he didn't say anything, just hefted her duffel bag from the truck and set it on the ground with the other supplies.

She tamped down her embarrassment at being caught drooling over him and stood up, crossing the short distance between them.

"What can I do to help?" she asked, fists stuffed into the pockets of her range jacket.

"Nothing," he said over his shoulder as he walked to the back of the horse trailer. "I've been through this so many times, I could unload and pack these horses in my sleep."

She watched again while he led two horses from the trailer, a big bay gelding and a smaller, sweet-looking paint mare. Without being asked, she grabbed the reins to hold the two so he could lead a third horse out. She tried not to smile back at his grateful grin, but couldn't stop the corners of her mouth from turning up.

It felt good being there, she thought, patting the big

bay. Like the paint, he dipped his head to munch the meadow grass.

"Sunny's the paint and the big guy is Rebel," Chase said from behind her, leading a sturdy buckskin mare. "One of the Lazy Jake kids called this one Bambi, and the name stuck."

"Hey, Sunny." Carly patted the paint's forelock, knowing instinctively that Rebel belonged to Chase.

Within minutes, working together in a companionable rhythm that needed few words, they had saddled and loaded the trio of horses.

Carly couldn't shake the sharp thrill of anticipation, mingled with no small degree of apprehension, that played through her as she mounted Sunny. She nudged the mare to follow Chase, with the packhorse hooked to Rebel's saddle, toward the trailhead. For now, Jackson brought up the rear of their little procession, but Carly didn't doubt that he'd soon take off on his own to menace any rabbits or chipmunks in the area.

She spent the first few minutes on the trail relearning the feel of a horse under her. It had been a few years since she'd done any riding, but she discovered it wasn't a skill easily forgotten. Her thighs quickly adjusted to Sunny's girth, and the reins felt as familiar in her hand as she suspected a fishing rod would.

On both sides of the trail the undergrowth was heavy and thick, lushly greened by the wet spring. The big pines filtered the sun for now, but Carly knew the trail would soon take them above the timberline, to places rocky and cold and harshly magnificent.

She shivered, already feeling the forces that were pulling her back to the deep wilderness, back to the wind-hewn mountain faces that were as familiar to her as her own face. She loved this gentler terrain they rode through now, with its wild geraniums and bright blue columbine. But her blood pumped faster, her senses seemed sharper, in the higher elevations, where patches of snow dotted the landscape like clotted cream.

Chase turned in his saddle a bit to watch her progress, and the expression on his face startled her. It must be a mirror of her own, she thought, that kind of respectful, anticipatory awe.

"So how long have you been doing this?" she asked. "Guiding, I mean."

"You afraid I might get you lost up there?"

"It wouldn't be the first time," she retorted.

He chuckled. "Come on, I was thirteen years old, for heaven's sake, and thought I was God's gift to mountaineering. When you're that age, you think you can do anything."

"Age has nothing to do with it. You *always* thought you could do anything." She smiled despite herself.

"Yeah, well, reality has a nasty way of slapping you around every once in a while." He tried to make it into a joke, but she caught a glimpse of something bleak in his eyes.

She suddenly wanted to distract him from whatever had put that look on his face. "You didn't answer my question. How long have you been doing this?"

"I started a couple of years after they took away my mitt and made me stop playing ball."

"Who is 'they'?"

"The team doctors and a whole busload of orthopedic specialists. They didn't really force me to quit, you understand, just sort of put things into perspective. After four patch-up jobs, I was told I ran the risk of blowing my knees out permanently if I stayed in the game. There I was, twenty-six years old—cocky as hell—and facing a choice of giving up the only thing I ever wanted to do with my life or spending the rest of it hobbling around on artificial knees."

"Tough choice."

"Yeah. A lot tougher at twenty-six than it looks here at thirty-one. It's hard for me to believe now, but as completely stupid as it sounds, I think I would have stayed in the game until I couldn't walk. The team took the decision out of my hands, though, by refusing to renew my contract. Catchers who can't crouch behind the plate aren't in too much demand." He gave a self-mocking laugh. "I think I enjoyed about fifteen sober minutes that first six months after I quit, until Jake came and dragged me home."

She tried to visualize him enduring painful operation after painful operation until he was forced to give up a life he loved. The image shook her. With dismay, she realized the emotion she felt was sorrow. Sorrow for Chase Samuelson? Why in heaven's name would it hurt so much to think of him that way?

She'd often told herself she wanted to see him suffer as she had, to know what it was like to be nearly destroyed by disillusionment. She felt no satisfaction now, just a fierce desire to cross the distance between them and wipe the disappointment from his eyes.

"What happened then?" she asked, stifling that inappropriate urge.

He fiddled with his reins. "After I came back to

Whiskey Creek, I saw Pop was restless on the ranch all by himself. He said he was tired of taking care of cattle and wanted to spend his retirement around people. Some of my buddies from the team had been out to fish and hunt at the Lazy Jake and they started pressuring me into doing something with it, so the whole idea of a lodge just clicked into place. Pop's in hog heaven over having new faces to tell all his old, worn-out stories to every week. It helped him get over Grandma's death too."

She could imagine Chase's grandpa loving it. The old man had always been full of pepper, as her dad used to say.

"Do *you* enjoy it?" she asked.

He turned toward her again, one hand resting on a powerful thigh, the other wrapped in the reins. He studied her for a moment, then one corner of his mouth quirked into a smile.

"Yeah. The kids make it all worth it."

Before she could ask him what kids he meant, he added quietly, "Sometimes I think it's as close to paradise as a guy like me is ever going to know. Like right now."

She held his gaze for one charged moment, then looked away, flustered by the intensity of his expression.

She had a sudden, passionate wish to forget about Mike, to relegate her anger to some tiny chamber in her mind, just for a while, and triple-padlock the door to keep it there. Wouldn't it be heavenly to explore this growing awareness between her and Chase without the underlying tension of their past?

For one brief, guilty moment, she considered the

pleasure of spending a day with Chase, accompanied only by the sounds of the wind blowing through the pines and the occasional call of a sharp-shinned hawk, instead of the angry chorus of disapproval that continued to ring through her conscience.

A cool breeze danced down the ridge, and she shivered, both from the cold and from remorse at her own disloyalty for even entertaining such a thought.

"It'll warm up in an hour or so," Chase said. Apparently he'd seen her shiver. "This time of year, it can be eighty degrees one minute, then turn into a blizzard the next."

"I remember."

"Of course you would."

"How often do you come up here?"

"Not as often as I'd like. I've got so much paperwork and fund-raising to do that I can only take time for about three or four week-long trips a season. Pop does most of the guiding, and the trips he can't take are handled by Tiny Mahoney and Clete Fletcher."

The names startled a laugh from Carly. "Clete and Tiny?" Two cowboys who could have written the book on being lazy and drunk except they were always too busy sleeping off their latest hangovers? "What are you doing with those two old bums?"

"They're my best ranch hands."

"You running a guide service or a halfway house?"

"Very funny." He grinned at her, and she had to force herself to look away from the brilliance of it. "For your information, little Miss smart-mouth, they've cleaned up their acts and you couldn't find two better guides in the whole county now. I'm lucky to have them."

"How did that happen?"

He shrugged, and on another man she would have said he looked embarrassed. "They just needed somebody to give them a chance. I gave them just what Pop gave me when he found me drunk and wrung out after the A's dropped me. A good talking-to, a few well-placed punches when things got ugly, and a new dream to work for."

"And it worked?"

"Like a charm."

Chase had worked some sort of charm over her, she thought. What else would give birth to these fluttery, flickering sensations that had no business creeping beneath her skin?

"We'd better get moving," she said, "if we want to make the halfway mark by nightfall."

Sunny responded to the light pressure Carly applied with her heels, and soon she was ahead of Chase on the trail, wishing she could outrun the feelings he'd stirred to life in her as easily.

With superhuman effort, Chase barely refrained from wincing as he watched Carly hobble into their campsite, Jackson close on her heels, back from washing up at the lake twenty feet away. Aching misery was obvious in every movement she made, from the tense set of her shoulders to the way she tried to prevent her thighs from touching each other as she walked.

Poor thing. She should have made him stop hours

ago. Any sensible woman wouldn't have insisted on toughing it out, when it was apparent it had been a while since she spent so much time on the back of a horse.

But then again, Carly Jacobs had never been the most sensible of females.

Here was another example of how she hadn't changed completely from the bright-eyed girl he'd known. She was still a dangerous mix of stubborn impulsiveness. He knew that the idiotic determination that had kept her glued to her horse when her muscles must have been crying out for relief would be his downfall. It would take a miracle for her to admit he hadn't been responsible for Mike's death. Something along the lines of an angelic visitation or a booming voice from the heavens bellowing his innocence might do the trick, but he doubted she'd even believe that, as staunchly as she clung to her convictions.

She limped into camp, pausing to take off her boots when she reached her tent, the tent she'd insisted be on the other side of the fire from his. From the look she'd given him when they were setting up camp, he figured she chose the location in order to stump any nefariously amorous plans he may have toward her: A midnight rendezvous would probably end with him tripping into the fire circle as he tried to sneak into her tent.

Where were angelic visitations when you really needed them? he wondered wryly.

She came back wearing a clean shirt, her hair freshly braided, just as he finished adding sliced potatoes, onions, peppers, and cheddar cheese to the bacon strips already sizzling in one of the Dutch ovens. She approached him slowly, moving as if her jeans had stiffened to about the consistency of concrete.

"Can I help you with anything?" she asked, and Chase grimaced at the whiteness of her face.

He should have been more observant, he thought. At the very least, he should have asked her that morning how much riding she'd done lately. Any other guest of Lazy Jake Outfitters would have received the third-degree about his or her experience on a horse, but he'd just assumed—since he knew she'd practically grown up on the back of a horse—that she still rode frequently.

Without even thinking about it, he'd pushed them all hard, until they'd covered more than half of the distance they needed to go.

His only excuse for not being more aware of her situation was his overwhelming preoccupation with the kiss they'd shared in his truck. Just remembering her sleepy murmurs and sweet response stirred his body to life. If he'd ever been more aroused by a simple kiss, he sure as heck couldn't remember it.

"Sit down, Carly, before you fall over," he ordered. Not unexpectedly, her eyes flashed fire and those luscious lips tightened.

"I'm fine, just a little stiff," she replied.

"How long since you've been on the back of a horse?"

"About an hour and thirteen minutes."

"Seriously, Carly. How long before today?"

She eased into one of the folding camp chairs. "The last time I had an assignment in a wilderness area, I guess, nearly two years ago. Most of the time we use good, old-fashioned pickups."

"Why didn't you swallow your damn pride and tell me you were hurting?"

"I'm fine," she repeated.

"The first-aid kit's got some medicated ointment that would take some of the sting out of your thighs. All you have to do is ask."

"And have you make some crack about how you're more than willing to rub it on for me? I'll pass, thanks."

"You've got a pretty high opinion of yourself, sweetheart, if you're afraid I want to jump your bones in your current condition," he blatantly lied. "I like my women to be able to move their legs a little more than three inches apart."

"To match their IQ level, I'm sure," she snapped.

He laughed, unoffended. The color was returning to her face with a vengeance, as he'd intended. Their verbal sparring didn't bother him. He'd have to be blind not to realize how stressful the day had been for her, and he just happened to be the most convenient outlet for that stress.

Besides, there were a lot worse things she could think about him than that he was a crass womanizer, even though that was about as far from the truth as a mule was from a Thoroughbred.

Come to think of it, there were a lot worse things she *did* believe about him. Taking his best friend's woman had to rank right up there. The reminder wiped the grin off his face, and he glumly finished preparing their dinner, then closed the lid and buried the dutch oven in the fire's ashes.

When he looked up, he saw Carly apparently had dismissed their heated barbs of a few minutes ago. Jackson lay silent at her feet, worn from his day of adventuring along the trail, and Chase would swear Carly looked almost relaxed.

"I'd forgotten how peaceful it can be up here." She smiled dreamily, and the little catch in his chest took him by surprise and left him feeling light-headed. Must be the altitude, he tried to tell himself, but deep inside, he suspected the truth. Somewhere between the past and the present, Carly had bewitched him with her flashing eyes and her fierce spirit, had begun to fill a place in him he'd only just realized was empty.

"I don't have much time to hike or camp just for sheer enjoyment anymore," she continued wistfully. "It seems like every time I'm up in the backcountry, I'm working, and I don't get much of a chance to appreciate it."

"What about fishing? You do much of that in Cheyenne?"

Her smile quickly straightened to a thin line. "Not much time for that, either."

"Come on, now, when was the last time you reeled in a rainbow?"

"Ten years ago," she answered shortly, turning away from him and looking as if she wished she hadn't said anything.

Ten years ago. When she was seventeen. When he'd left town with Jessie. When Mike had self-destructed. What a hell of a mess.

"Well, Miz Jacobs, if you don't mind me saying so, I think ten years is a mighty long time to go without wetting a line. Bad for the soul, don't you know."

She didn't answer him, just continued staring off into the distance.

"Yep, that explains a lot of things." He put his hands on his knees to rise. He walked toward their gear, stowed under a rain flap attached to his tent.

He knew he took a big risk goading her, but at the same time he had the strangest feeling that if he could get her to the water's edge with a rod and reel in her hand, it would be the first step in regaining her trust.

"Explains what?" she asked.

"Nothing. Just thinking aloud." He pulled out a thick black tube from one of the saddlebags.

She studied it for a moment, then turned to him, her eyes filled with accusation. "Put it away, Chase. I'm not fishing with you."

"Why not? You need something to help you unwind after your tough commute today. Dinner won't be ready for another hour, your dog's too tuckered to play, and I suspect your body's too sore to go hiking. The only alternative is to sit here and stare at each other. As much as that appeals to me, I'm pretty sure it wouldn't interest you too much."

"You're crazy, you know that? It's going to be pitch-dark in less than an hour."

"Great. That gives us less than an hour to catch our limits, so hurry it up."

"Chase . . ."

He ignored her, opening the tube and drawing out both his well-used Winston fly rod and the spare pack combination rod.

Over her shoulder, a thousand brilliant flickers on

the lake caught his gaze, and his hands froze on the fishing gear.

"Take a look at the water," he commanded Carly softly.

The sun, in its last big burst of color before setting behind the mountains, rode the far horizon in a blaze of lavender and pink and peach. It was an awe-inspiring sight, magnified by the reflection cast on the shimmering alpine lake.

And everywhere color touched the water, a bubbling symphony of movement could be seen, like a huge boiling cauldron in some cosmic production of Shakespeare's *Macbeth*. Dusk was prime feeding time for the cold-water trout, and he watched them leaping above the surface, looking for the juiciest insects, their silver bellies catching the sunset and breaking it into sharp flashes of light.

Though Chase had seen the sight hundreds of times before, at other lakes in other mountains, the dance of survival never failed to stir him, to jumble his priorities until they rearranged themselves in solid, centered order.

He took a deep breath, sucking in the familiar, beguiling smell and taste of the place. It was at times like this, with the sharp tang of pine mingling with the wet scent of life rising off the lake, that he felt no regret for the career he'd lost.

Sure, the baseball field had offered its own unique assault to the senses. The smell of leather oil and metal from the catcher's mask. The sweetness of freshly mowed grass. The raw power of human sweat and surging adrenaline, of fifty thousand people yelling and stomping and pouring energy into him until he felt he would burst with it.

It had been heady and addicting, and sometimes he missed it so badly he wanted to pound his fists into a tree until his knuckles bled, channeling the fierce ache into something physical.

But it only took a sight like a sunset feeding on a glacial lake to put things in perspective.

Life in the Major Leagues was a transitory, elusive thing, too easily lost. He, of all people, knew that. This, however, would go on long after the last baseball player had hung up his cleats and thrown away his glove.

He dared a look at Carly and saw her staring at the lake as if hypnotized, clear longing battling with what looked like fear in her expressive, sooty eyes.

It was almost as if she were thinking the same thought that had crossed his mind: Fishing with him would mean crossing some internal threshold of trust.

He realized he was holding his breath as he waited for her to make the first move, and he let it out in a rush. As he watched, suspicion won the upper hand in her inner struggle and she turned away from the water.

"Come on, Carly Jane. What are you afraid of? Me? Yourself?" He spoke softly, like a boy trying to coax a wild animal into taking a morsel of food from his fingers. She froze at his words, her face averted, and he continued in what he hoped was a low, nonthreatening tone. "Would it be so awful to sit beside me for a few minutes while the sun is setting and the fish are rising? If you want, I'll even put the nasty old worm on your hook so you don't have to get your pretty little hands dirty."

She sent him a look of disgust, then realized he was

joking. A reluctant smile tugged at her delectable mouth. They both knew she'd probably live-baited more hooks than he had, even with her decade-long hiatus. He was strictly a dry-fly angler, a skill she'd never mastered.

He tried one more time, as close to begging as he could bring himself. "Last one to set a hook gets stuck with the supper dishes."

She sat there for a few more seconds, an errant wind twisting and wrapping stray sun-kissed curls around her jaw. He realized he was holding his breath again, but this time his lungs refused to exhale while he awaited her decision. He wanted her to take the rod from him more than he remembered ever wanting anything else.

The moments dragged on and the sun slipped another notch on the horizon. Then, just when he thought she would turn away again, she smiled faintly and grabbed the rod.

FIVE

Years later, if Carly were asked to list the truly perfect moments in her life, fishing with Chase Samuelson on a cool summer evening deep in the primitive Wind Rivers would have to top the list.

The only sounds were the wind singing through the pines and the occasional splash from a trout rising above the mirrored surface of the lake. A huge moon rose early, outshining the dying rays of the sun and casting its unearthly half-light over the landscape. And Chase stood on the bank beside her, pausing every once in a while to aim a conspiratorial grin in her direction, as if they were grade-schoolers ditching a math test together.

It was a magical, surrealistic trip through time to a childhood filled with peace and laughter, and she wanted to clutch it tightly, selfishly, to her chest.

When she'd picked up the rod and made that first cast into the water with trembling, unpracticed hands, Carly thought for sure Chase would be able to see how rattled she felt. But he just smiled and moved on down the shore a bit, as if to give her privacy to compose herself. Could he sense how important this was? she wondered. Did he know she'd longed for years to be doing this very thing but had always chickened out.

Once, a year after Mike's death, she'd gathered her fishing gear and headed toward the old Standby. She'd craved the peace she always found at the water's edge and had been positive she was mature enough, that she had her emotions under control enough, to be able to deal with it.

She hadn't even been able to get out of the car.

She remembered sitting there for a good hour, Mike's beat-up old tackle box in hand, fighting tears and loss and memories. Finally she'd thrown the damn box against a tree and watched while swivels and flies and rolls of six-pound nylon leader spilled out like the insides of a gutted fish.

Hours later, she'd returned with a flashlight to clean up the mess, but she'd never been able to summon the courage to try again.

Until now.

She shivered, more from the memory twisting around inside her than from the chill as the sun snatched its warmth away. Chase must have caught the motion, for he reeled his line in and crossed the space between them.

"You doing all right?" He stood there awkwardly, as if he wanted to say more.

She managed a shaky smile. "Well, I haven't caught any hooks in my hair yet with this atrocious casting, if that's what you're asking."

"Dinner should be just about ready by now. I can

bring you a plate here or we can eat in camp, if you don't want to do this anymore."

She really should quit now, she thought, but it seemed too precious, like finding a forgotten box stuffed full of memories in the corner of the attic. "I—I'd like to stay."

His answer was a quick smile she couldn't help returning.

A few minutes later he sauntered back balancing a plate of food on each hand, a gray flannel shirt tucked under one arm.

"I didn't know where to find your jacket, so I just grabbed something of mine." He set one of the plates on the rock next to her and handed her the shirt.

"This is fine. Thank you." It was better than fine. It was heavenly, almost like an embrace. She successfully fought the urge to rub her cheek against the soft fabric but couldn't help inhaling the scent of him that clung to it, a heady mix of pine and leather and sky.

She glanced up, trying to shake off the purely sensuous experience, only to find Chase staring at her with a completely unguarded expression on his face of wistful longing and stark desire. Their eyes locked, and for an instant the idyllic surroundings blurred and faded around her, like an old photograph exposed to too much sunlight. Only his image pierced the haze, strong and masculine, dearly familiar.

"Chase? Thank you," she whispered.

"For the shirt? Don't worry about it." He grinned. "Believe me, it looks better on you than it ever could on me."

"For the shirt, and for . . . everything else. I've missed this."

She waited for an "I told you so," but Chase just smiled with genuine delight. He pulled two cans of beer from his back pockets, making her wonder how he'd shoved them back there, as tight as his faded jeans fit. He tossed one to her, then grabbed the other plate of food and picked a boulder to stretch out on a few feet from her.

Carly felt lightened somehow, warmed by both his shirt and his easy smile.

It was as painful as a toothache to admit, she thought, picking at the plate of food, but maybe her mother was right. Maybe Chase was a decent human being after all. The problem was, how did she reconcile this man quietly whistling the theme to the old *Andy Griffith* TV show with the villain she had imagined him to be for all these years?

Did she even want to try?

The hurt and bitterness seemed so distant now, like the farthest star among the massive light show pinpricking the heavens, and Carly found the idea of dredging it all up again distinctly abhorrent. It would simplify the rest of their trip if she just took a pragmatic approach to their past.

The Chase she blamed for her brother's death couldn't share the same skin as the man who generated these sweet, alive feelings in her. Chase seemed to have matured into a man who cared about others, a man who went to the trouble of straightening up two of the laziest degenerates around, who brought groceries to snowbound widows.

If he had been reckless and selfish when he was twenty-one, she mused, it wasn't that unusual at an age when people tend to think they were invincible anyway. Add to that natural spit-in-your-eye cockiness an obscenely lucrative contract with the A's, and was it really so surprising that Chase had thought he could take what, or whom, he wanted, regardless of the consequences to those left behind?

Carly sighed, and Chase glanced at her quizzically.

"Everything okay?" he asked.

"Mmmmm. Just thinking."

"It's the thin air at this altitude. Makes your brain work faster." He smiled, a slow, lazy smile, and Carly felt shaky from more than just the scarce oxygen.

"That must be it," she mumbled.

"Best kind of therapy around. Much better than any big-city, two-hundred-dollar-an-hour, blame-everything-on-your-parents shrink."

"Is that the voice of experience?"

"Not me. I'm pretty happy where I am right now. Who wouldn't be? I work with the best people on earth, surrounded by the most stunning scenery God has to offer, and on my own schedule. Not bad for a dumb Wyoming cowboy."

"What about you?" Chase asked. "You must get some kind of charge taking the guns away from the bad guys."

"Sometimes I really hate it," she answered vehemently.

He looked startled. "What do you hate? The job?"

She tossed a rock into the water, watching the circles expand until they disappeared. "No. It's all this needless killing, just for a few dollars or, worse, for a trophy to hang on the wall of some rich guy's den. It can leave a real bad taste in the mouth after a while."

"Why do it? If it makes you unhappy, do something else."

"I'm not unhappy. I love being a game warden. It's all I've ever wanted to do."

He chuckled. "That's right. When you weren't following me and Mike around, you were always traipsing after Verl."

"There's a lot I enjoy about it: studying rare animals in their natural habitat, not being tied to a desk, the camaraderie with the guys. I especially love the detective work."

"But . . . ?" he prompted.

"Sometimes it can be overwhelming."

Overwhelming? It could be downright dehumanizing, she thought. She'd seen hunters who killed scores of nesting waterfowl in a day, just for target practice. She'd seen boys not even old enough to drive a car exhibit no remorse at all for blasting away at anything that moved, whether it was in season or not. More times than she cared to consider, she'd spent weeks on a case, only to see the perps plead their way down through the courts and get off with a few months' probation or a piddling amount of community service.

"Poaching is all about greed," she said, "about taking something that belongs to no one and everyone at the same time. And then desecrating it in the most heinous way possible, hacking off a paw here or some antlers there, gouging out the insides, then leaving the rest to rot."

She threw another stone into the lake. "How can I give up that feeling, naive as it may be, that I've been able to make the world a little better, that I've protected something sacred and vital to all of us? How can I . . ." Her voice trailed off when she finally caught the expression in his eyes, amusement mingled with something she couldn't quite name.

She felt heat rush to her cheeks. "Sorry. I tend to get a little . . . zealous when it comes to wildlife conservation. I didn't mean to bore you."

"Don't apologize for caring about what you do. Mike would have been as proud of you as I am."

If possible, she felt her face flush even more, but she couldn't deny the spurt of ridiculous pleasure that settled over her at his praise like a soft July rain.

Setting her plate aside, Carly picked up the fishing rod again, suddenly eager to use the remaining few minutes of light. Warm and sated and free of the last hard nuggets of tension that had been with her all day, she relaxed on the rocky bank, lulled by the song of the wind and the water.

She must have dozed off for a while. When she returned to consciousness it was to a world of peace and comfort. It took her a minute to realize why—Chase had pulled her into his arms while she slept. She was cradled to his chest, her back to him, his chin resting on her hair.

She closed her eyes again, helpless against the heady, wholly unaccustomed sensation of being cherished. Could she somehow stay like this until morning, she wondered, tucked against his strength, safe from the harshness of real life? No, she thought. Already her body was responding to the proximity of his potent masculinity. Any minute now, she'd be turning in his arms and pressing her mouth to his, unable to fight the current of desire that would surely suck her down if she gave into her growing need for him.

Breaking the contact between them was the hardest thing she'd ever done, but she summoned all her willpower and sat up, brushing the hair from her face. Had she pulled it from the braid or had he?

"How long have I been—" she couldn't stop the jaw-popping yawn that interrupted her, "asleep?"

What she recognized as regret darkened his eyes to a navy blue. "Not long enough. I think you've had just about all the fun you can handle in one night."

The horses nickered softly as they walked the few yards back to camp, and Jackson thumped his tail on the ground where he'd curled near the dying embers in the fire ring.

Chase dropped the fishing gear near his tent and followed her across the camp to her own, hands at his sides and a distracted frown wrinkling his forehead.

Was it her imagination or did he seem as shaken by the evening as she was? Carly wondered.

He bent to unzip the tent for her, then faced her again. "Will you be warm enough? It's still early in the season and the nights usually dip below freezing."

She nodded, touched by his concern. "I've got a good sleeping bag. You?"

"I should be fine. Thanks."

They stood there awkwardly for a few moments. Finally, Chase reached out a hand and twisted a stray tendril of hair around his finger. His tenderness completely disarmed her, and without thinking, Carly stepped forward to give him a quick, instinctive hug, to thank him for giving her back something so precious.

His arms slid around her and they stood motionless in the embrace, the heat of their bodies shimmering between them. For the second time that night, the world around Carly receded, bringing only Chase into sharp focus.

She waited, hypnotized, for his mouth to descend, for the passion that hovered around them like the voracious flames of a forest fire to engulf them with its heat. From far off she heard the distinctive hoot of a great horned owl, but the only thing that had meaning was the man who held her, the one she'd handed her heart to years ago.

Just before he kissed her she wondered if maybe he'd never bothered to give it back.

From the sizzling sensations zinging between them, she had expected a passionate kiss, the frenzied meshing of lips and tongues and teeth. The reality was far, far gentler, so stirringly sweet, it brought tears to her eyes.

Chase brushed his lips against hers three, maybe four times, then she heard him whisper her name against her hair as he tightened his hold. She could feel her heart racing wildly, in stark contrast to the tender quiet of the moment. Or maybe it was his heart. They stayed locked in the embrace, both silent, while clouds danced across the full moon.

"I've missed you, Carly," he said hoarsely. "It never hit me how damn much until you came back to town. What would I have to do to win back even a little of that friendship we used to have?"

Take me fishing, she almost said. *Hold me and warm me*

and wash away the past. But fear strangled the words in her throat, and she simply tightened her hold around his waist.

After a few more minutes, she felt his lips on her hair again, then he was pulling away. She rubbed her arms at the sudden chill. Despite the aches in her body and the exhaustion that nearly blurred her vision, she didn't want this day to end. She had a terrible fear that when she awoke in the morning, this fragile tenderness would be gone, leaving only the bitterness she had carried for too many years.

Chase tucked a strand of hair behind her ear and smiled that lopsided grin before turning away.

"Sweet dreams, darlin'," he called softly as he walked to his tent. "Sweet dreams."

Muffled swearing from somewhere outside her tent woke Carly the next morning. Her internal clock—and the dimness inside the tent—suggested the sun wouldn't be sliding over the mountains for at least another half-hour.

She stretched as much as she could in the jumbled-up sleeping bag, then winced as her body vociferously reminded her of the beating it had taken the day before. Muscles she'd forgotten about burned in her legs and bottom. Her muffled groan produced a tiny cloud of steam that obscured her vision, then quickly dissolved. Carly willed her body to quit complaining so she could figure out why Chase would be cussing up a storm this early in the morning.

Smiling widely as the curses became more imaginative and explicit, she reached for the clothes she'd placed at the bottom of her sleeping bag to keep them moderately warm. Despite the aches in her body and the chilly air, she was surprised at how refreshed she felt. Being in the mountains with Chase felt so . . . so . . . What? she wondered.

Entertaining? Yes. Exhilarating? Definitely. But it was something deeper.

Right, she realized. It felt right and exactly what it was, a sweet reunion of two people who had been separated by far more than just years and distance.

She quickly slipped on her jeans and boots and groped through the dark tent for a shirt—his, she realized, but she slipped it on anyway, over the long underwear she'd slept in.

The chilly air inside the tent hadn't prepared her for the breath-stealing cold that assaulted her when she opened the flap and stepped out. An arctic wind slapped her in the face before dancing quickly away. Carly gasped at the sting, then stood frozen by far more than the cold at the sight that greeted her across the campsite.

Chase, dressed only in a pair of unbuttoned jeans that rode low on his hips, was standing next to the fire wiping a towel across his bare chest. Drops of moisture clung to the skin that stretched tight over hard muscles, and his dark hair was tousled and wet.

Carly gulped. A fully dressed Chase wreaked havoc on her nervous system. This half-naked version was positively lethal.

She must have made some sound, because he turned just as she was willing the circulation back to her extremities. He waved the towel at her.

"Mornin'."

"Uh, hello," she managed.

He turned his back to her and fastened his jeans. "Sorry if I woke you. I'd planned to let you get at least another hour of sleep."

She walked over to the fire and its warmth. A delicious aroma curled out of a blue spatterware coffeepot on the coals, telling her he'd already been busy this morning. She pulled the sleeve of his shirt down over her hand to prevent burned fingers and gripped the pot's handle, then inhaled deeply as she poured the coffee into a matching mug.

"I'm glad you did. Wake me, I mean," she said, after the first magnificent sip. Why did coffee always taste better made on a campfire? "I slept like a rock."

"I slept *on* a rock," he muttered. "I had about a dozen boulders with my name on 'em under my sleeping bag."

Carly tried not to laugh. "What a whiner. In all the years we camped together, you never woke up in a good mood."

"Yeah, that's because Mike snored loud enough to wake a deaf dog, while you always managed to get a tent all by yourself!"

"Ha! Don't blame me, mister." She took another sip. "You guys just wanted me out of the way so you could talk about things like how you felt-up Annie Roskelley in the backseat of your granddaddy's old Torino after the Fourth of July picnic."

Chase frowned fiercely as he slipped on a fresh blue chamois shirt. "How the Sam Hill did you know about that?"

She could swear his ears turned red. "Sound waves travel awfully well at these high altitudes. And tent walls don't do a whole lot to slow them down."

He snorted. "It's bad manners to eavesdrop on conversations that don't concern you, little girl."

This time she couldn't help the laugh that escaped, any more than she could resist the urge to tease him. "I don't think you'd pass any etiquette classes, the way you two discussed the young lady in question, Chase. If I remember right, you were raving about a part of her anatomy that was, I quote, 'as choice as Grandma's prizewinning beefsteak tomatoes.' "

He moved behind her so fast she didn't have time to react. Before she knew it, one muscled arm had snaked around her neck, drawing her back against his hard chest. The knuckles of his other hand were pressed against her hair, poised to deliver a noogie, just the way both he and her brother used to give her with disgusting regularity.

"You ought to be ashamed of yourself, Carly Jacobs," he said sternly, amidst her gasping struggles to free herself without spilling the hot coffee. "I was only seventeen years old, after all, and it hurts me deeply that you'd stoop low enough to taunt me with a single act of passion that brings me nothing but shame now that I'm older and wiser."

"Ha!" She gave up both the effort to get away and to hold in her laughter when she caught him fighting his own grin. "If you live to be a hundred years old, I don't think you could ever be ashamed of that golden moment, just you and the fireworks and a braless Annie

Roskelley. You were a bad, bad boy, Chase. All the mothers in town except mine thought so."

He squeezed her tighter, unleashing zillions of little hormones to run crazily through her insides.

"I just want to know how you have such perfect recollection of a brief conversation that must have happened nearly fifteen years ago," he said, releasing her and moving away to pour coffee into a second mug.

"Yeah, well, I've always been a sucker for bad boys," Carly muttered, then felt her face flame as she realized how much she'd revealed through her words.

"Anyway," she quickly went on, changing the subject, "what was all the commotion this morning? You step on a porcupine or something?"

"Close. That blasted dog of yours. He followed me to the lake while I washed up, and he must have thought I needed a real bath."

"Oh no." A vision of Chase plummeting into the water flashed across her mind and she stifled a grin. "He didn't push you in, did he?"

"Not exactly. Just sort of gave me a friendly nudge and the slick rocks and my bad knees did the rest. I strongly advise against any refreshing dips in the lake this morning, unless you want to freeze off parts of you that may come in handy later in life."

He looked endearingly disgruntled, and Carly was stunned by the wave of tenderness that washed over her. The dirty look he gave her dog when Jackson trotted happily into camp just then elicited a spontaneous laugh from her, which, for the sake of diplomacy, she tried to hide behind a cough. An apology was definitely in order, she decided.

"Jack, come here," she ordered in the voice their beleaguered obedience trainer had assured her would net instant results. The big hound looked at her goofily, then ambled over, nose quivering in expectation of a treat. Aware Chase was watching, Carly grabbed the dog's chin and forced it up gently. "You owe Mr. Samuelson an apology. Go tell him you're sorry for making him be so clumsy. Go on. I think that's what he's waiting for before he'll fix our breakfast." She choked down another laugh as Chase backed away.

"No really," he said as the dog trotted eagerly toward him. "This isn't necessary. No hard feelings."

He aimed a desperate glance her way. "Carly, call him off. Please!"

"No way," she answered, straight-faced. "He needs to be taught a lesson." She couldn't stop her laugh when all eighty pounds of her dog stood on his hind legs, planted his massive paws on Chase's shoulders, and began energetically licking his whisker-shadowed cheeks.

"Carly!" He tried to ward off the dog, but Jack never could be swayed when he had his mind set on something. Carly finally took pity on Chase and produced a dog biscuit to lure the overgrown puppy away from his new best friend. The dog gulped it down and sauntered over to the fire to await his breakfast.

Chase grabbed the towel he'd been using to dry himself and swiped at his face. "Ugh. Dog germs," he moaned, just like Lucy in the Charlie Brown comics whenever Snoopy got too close.

"What are you complaining about?" Carly teased. "It was just a little good-morning kiss."

He flicked the towel at her, like he used to do with

wet dish towels when he spent the night at their house and Betsy would make the boys help clean up the kitchen after supper.

In reflex, she grabbed the end before it reached her, then emitted a startled cry when he jerked the towel—and her—toward him. "How 'bout an apology along those same lines from the lady who sicced that hound from hell on me?"

His arms slid around her, and despite her better judgment Carly relaxed into him. With a boldness that surprised her, she tilted her head to look at him, then shyly kissed one stubbled cheek, reveling in the sandpaper texture against her sensitive lips. "I'm so sorry, sir," she said breathlessly, "that you can't manage to keep your legs under you."

"Not when you're around, anyway," he muttered just before he kissed her.

It was everything she had expected the night before and more. Leftover passion quickly flared to bright, vivid life, rocking her to her very center. With strong fingers, he gripped the nape of her neck through her unbound hair, holding her a willing captive while his mouth played a magic song on hers, nipping and sucking at her lips until her knees weakened and her hands tangled in the soft fabric of his untucked shirt.

She was only dimly aware of the world around them, of the fire popping, of the birds waking the mountain with their morning songs. She knew only the taste of Chase, only the sound of their rapid breathing, only the shifting and settling of her heart.

When she loved him all those years ago, she'd been too young to know about the passion a man and a woman could spark between them, about this nameless burning ache that swept away all thought, leaving a yearning that only one man could fill. Nothing in her life had prepared her for this, for the trembling of her limbs and the way she couldn't seem to catch her breath. The sharp intensity of feeling thrilled her at the same time it frightened her with its force. She summoned whatever vestiges of willpower she had left and pulled away, awed by the passion blazing from his eyes.

Somehow, she managed a shaky smile, trying to let him know without words that her withdrawal wasn't a rejection, just a bid for time to get used to these wild cravings.

He seemed to understand. After a few moments, he returned her smile. "As much as I'd like to spend all morning doing this," he said, "I guess we'd best get going. We've got a lot of trail to cover if you plan on hitting Mitchell Springs by nightfall."

She nodded, already regretting that she'd stopped them.

SIX

Chase refused to let himself grow too optimistic.

As they rode deeper into the wilderness, Carly seemed to drop more of her coolness toward him, until she was laughing and teasing and stopping frequently to drink in the sheer beauty of the increasingly harsh landscapes where the patches of snow became more frequent and the trees more scarce. It was as if the years of silence between them had been nothing more than a passing irritation.

Frankly, her softened attitude terrified him senseless.

Each time she flashed that spontaneous grin his way, he wanted to tumble them both off their horses and take her hard and fast, right there in the dirt.

He'd always considered himself a fairly liberated guy. His grandma could rope and ride as well as any hand they'd ever had, and growing up with two devious-minded sisters had taught him early that women were far from the gentle sex society still tended to depict them as.

After word of the Annie Roskelley incident somehow

filtered back to his grandfather, Jake had taken him aside and given him a stern lecture about how women wanted to be treated. At the time, Chase had thought it unfair to be bawled out for talking about something the girl had instigated, but Jake had used tough words.

"Don't matter who they are or what they may do with themselves or their bodies," Chase clearly remembered him saying, a ruddy blush coloring his grizzled cheeks. "You treat all women like you want other fellas to treat your little sisters and you'll get along just fine."

Even with his adolescent hormones blazing, he'd recognized it as sound advice and had remembered the lecture frequently over the years.

Thanks to Jake's lecture, he'd never been able to bring himself to play the game some of his teammates perfected—picking a different groupie to share their beds every night. At first, he'd been too busy with Jessie and her problems to have time for another woman. After she was settled, he found he had little interest in the women who hung out at the ballpark. And they were more interested in his batting average and his bank balance than him.

He'd gravitated toward women he met outside of baseball, and the few serious relationships he'd had were established on common interests, cemented by friendship and affection.

That was one of the reasons why his primitive, visceral reaction to Carly astounded him. He'd never experienced such gut-twisting, scorching desire for a woman. It made him sweat and ache and adjust himself every few minutes to try to get more comfortable in the saddle.

She was beautiful, he couldn't deny that. Even in

blue jeans and the bright scarlet cotton shirt of the Game and Fish Department, she looked fresh and clean. Sunlight caressed and surrounded her, glinting off her magnificent hair so brightly, it hurt his eyes to look at her. Not that a little eye burn was keeping him from staring at her as frequently as he dared. Watching her was like gazing straight into the sun at high noon, but, by damn, he'd take his chances. He planned to look his fill, even if it blinded him.

When it came right down to bare facts, he couldn't help himself.

Some inner force kept him tuned to each movement she made: every time she smiled his mouth went dry; whenever she arched her head back and her chest out to stretch stiff muscles, he gritted his teeth. He nearly poured his canteen over his head when she leaned forward to pat Sunny, her pert behind in the air while she half stood in the stirrups.

Okay, it had been a while since he was intimate with a woman. A long, long while, to be honest, since he'd even been interested in expending the energy it took for a serious relationship. Still, he'd barely noticed the lack of any romantic entanglements in his life until a certain chocolate-eyed woman returned to town to haunt his dreams and torment his waking hours.

What scared him, Chase reflected grimly, wasn't the physical currents that zinged between them. He could deal with those, even if they temporarily made life a little uncomfortable.

No, what had him quaking in his size 14 boots went deeper than a few hormones.

He was very much afraid he was in love with her.

This wasn't the confused heat of a baffled twenty-one-year-old burning for a girl-woman who set him on fire with a laughing glance. Yeah, there had definitely been something there ten years ago. He'd respected her grit, enjoyed her sense of humor, been proud of the way she stood up for herself back then, even when she was a teenager.

This, though, was a man's love, strong and sure and ferocious. He wanted to take her inside of him, to absorb her wit and her courage, to spend the rest of his life trying to bring out that sweet, hesitant smile.

Who was he kidding? Chase thought glumly. There was more chance of palm trees growing in the Wyoming wilderness than there was of Carly ever sharing his love.

She felt something for him. He'd seen it in her eyes both the night before outside her tent, and again that morning; a kind of scared vulnerability that had stunned him. But he was caught in a catch-22. She might be attracted to him, but she would never love him completely, not when she believed he was the kind of man who could turn his back on a lifelong friendship, who would snatch Jessie right out of Mike's hands.

If he told her the truth about that spring, though, she'd eventually come to hate him for shattering all her beliefs about Mike. Carly had so few things left of the brother she'd adored, but at least she still carried a precious fistful of joyous memories. How could he run the risk of stealing those away from her too?

"Hey, scout. Wait up." Her call from a few hundred feet behind him jolted him from the thought. He turned quickly, wincing and inhaling sharply as a familiar, ragged pain sliced from the worse of his bum knees. After the quick shock of pain, he ignored the steady throbbing by force of long habit.

"Sorry," he called back, reining in Rebel. He'd let the distance between them grow, and it took her a couple of minutes to catch up.

"Some guide you are," she teased. "I could have been lunch for a mountain lion and you wouldn't even have noticed I was gone."

"Are you kidding?" he bantered back. "Any self-respecting cougar would recognize that shirt of yours by the glare and know you're a sainted guardian of the animal kingdom. He wouldn't dare touch you for fear of bringing down the wrath of the whole forest."

"Don't spread that manure quite so thick. I'm only wearing hiking boots, not hip waders."

"What?" He grinned. "Are you questioning my sincerity?"

"Not at all. My mother always claimed you could charm an angry grizzly into handing over her cub, and get her to smile while she did it."

"Your mother vastly overestimates the extent of my charm, if my success with you is anything to go by," Chase muttered.

Carly gave him a sidelong glance, the corners of her mouth quirking up. "Oh, I wouldn't say that. You seem to be doing a pretty good job so far."

He blinked, stunned into speechlessness. What did she mean by that? He fumbled for an answer, but apparently she'd decided she said enough. She spurred Sunny into a trot, and she and the horse were twenty yards ahead of him before he managed to shut his mouth.

Conversation was scarce between them for the remainder of the day. They stopped for a brief lunch on the trail, both of them pushing hard to reach Mitchell Springs.

With frequent glances that he hoped were inconspicuous, Chase watched her expression shift and change as she tried to work out what they both knew was happening between them. He saw confusion and wariness and myriad other emotions slide across her face.

How the hell did a man know what to do with a woman who acted like she hated him one moment and like she wanted to curl up in his sleeping bag the next?

The weird thing was, he thought, he could deal with an angry Carly a whole heckuva lot better than the soft, vulnerable woman she'd been that morning and last night, her lips wet from his kisses, her eyes dewy with need.

When she was spitting and clawing at him, he knew he could poke and prod and tease until she was laughing despite herself. But when she looked at him with her soul shining in those incredible brown eyes, he couldn't decide whether to climb to a nearby mountain peak and yell his elation to the world or run and hide in the closest cave for fear of hurting her.

He settled for riding along stoically behind her, sneaking peeks and hoping like hell his bad knees wouldn't do anything to disgrace him in front of her.

Rebel's anxious nickering distracted Chase from his musings, and he frowned to realize the air had grown heavy with moisture, with dark thunderclouds gathering ominously above them. Even the chattering of the magpies had stilled and the whole wilderness seemed hushed, holding its collective breath for the impending storm.

A sudden gust of cold wind had him grabbing for his baseball cap, and he cursed himself for being so preoccupied that he hadn't noticed the weather changing. To complicate matters, they'd begun descending the last big mountain between them and their destination, and the narrow trail snaked and hairpinned treacherously on this section, hugging the side of the hill like a wispy piece of string.

He was trying to figure out the best way to get them all to shelter before those mean-looking clouds unleashed their fury, when lightning arced not sixty feet from them, slicing with an earsplitting crack into a spruce tree off the trail.

Carly jumped in surprise, and Jackson yelped and ran across the trail toward them with his tail tucked between his legs as thunder growled loud and long. The horses whinnied and stamped anxiously, and Chase felt his heart skip a beat when the normally placid Sunny side-stepped closer to the steep drop-off.

"Easy," he called softly, but Carly had already regained control. She eased the horse toward safety as huge dollops of rain began plopping around them.

Another lightning bolt struck uncomfortably close and was quickly followed by three more, scattered across the mountainside. "Any great ideas, scout?" Carly asked nervously.

"Sure. Let's try to stay dry."

"Brilliant. That must be why you're in charge."

"Exactly."

"What about the lightning? We can't pitch tents in this."

He glanced around, trying to gain his bearings, then turned back to her with relief.

"How do you feel about caves?" He had to yell to be heard over the thunder that crashed and rolled in a constant rumble.

"They've always been among my favorite geologic formations," she yelled back. "Why?"

"I found one not too far from here a few summers ago. We're close enough to Mitchell Springs that we can set up camp there."

"Let's move then."

Chase led the way, while the skies spat angrily at them, the rain piercing through their clothing with chilling force.

A few yards from the cave, Chase stopped them, pulling from his saddle bag a flashlight and the long, wickedly sharp knife he used to gut fish. "Stay here," he ordered Carly. The last thing he needed was her going one-on-one with some wild critter that might be using this cave for a cozy home.

Carly grimaced as Chase walked toward the mouth of the cave without waiting for an answer. He was so arrogantly sure she would obey that she followed out of sheer stubbornness.

"No, thanks all the same," she mumbled, trailing him to the opening in the rock, no bigger than the length of one of their horses.

He turned, scowling, at her approach. "Dammit, Carly, go back with the horses. Last summer I saw bear sign around here, and I don't particularly care to watch you wrestle a half ton of angry mama bear today."

"There's no bear."

"How can you be so sure?"

"You're the guide, look around. No fresh tracks, no droppings, no recent claw marks on the trees. Besides, Jack wouldn't be so calm. He has a nervous breakdown if he gets within a few miles of one."

It took Chase a few minutes of stubborn male determination to look around and discover she was right. Strange, she thought, but she didn't feel like rubbing his nose in it. It was kind of sweet, actually, Chase's way of looking out for her, just like in the old days.

"I bow to your superior knowledge," he finally said, and shone the flashlight into the yawning mouth of the mountain.

She had to stoop to enter an area that was no bigger than her mother's living room. It wasn't a cave in the truest sense of the word, with no mysterious passageways that begged to be explored. It was more like a horizontal slit in the mountain. A closed, musty stench assailed her, and the temperature was cold enough to make her breath puff out. But it was unquestionably better than taking their chances putting up the tents while deadly lightning flashed around outside.

Something furry and warm brushed against her legs, and she couldn't stop an instinctive squeak. Chase quickly turned the flashlight on her, and chuckled at the sight of Jackson trying to snuggle into Carly's warmth.

"Don't scare me like that again, you hear?" He sounded relieved, and again she felt a quick spurt of warmth at his concern.

"If you two can stay out of trouble," he went on, "I'm going to hobble the horses and grab some of our gear, and maybe find some dry wood."

"Don't worry about us. You be careful out there. That lightning isn't letting up."

In the dim light, she watched a dimple appear as Chase held out the flashlight to her.

"I've got a few more of these in one of the packs. You take this one and use it to clobber any big, hairy beasts who might wander in out of the rain."

"You mean, besides you?"

"Ha, ha." The dimple appeared again, and as Carly reached to take the flashlight, her hand touched his for just an instant. It was the first time their flesh had connected since their heated kiss of that morning, and she was unable to control her shiver. She instinctively jerked the flashlight away.

Chase inhaled deeply and let his breath out in a long sigh. "You know we're going to have to talk about this, don't you, sweetheart?"

"About . . . what?"

"The fact that every time I touch you, you either jump like you're terrified I'm going to belt you one, or shiver like you want me to make love with you until you can't think straight."

His frankness elicited a startled laugh from her, and she shone the light into his face. "I think you've taken one too many wild pitches to the head, Samuelson. You think every woman you meet wants a quick roll in the hay?"

"No," he answered quietly. "There's more going on here than just chemistry, more than just one hell of a physical attraction. I can tell you sense it as strongly as I do."

She was grateful she was the one holding the light, so

he couldn't see her blush. "The only thing going on here is I'm freezing, I'm dripping wet, and I'm tired."

He watched her for a moment, then shrugged. "Have it your way. You've been fighting me for ten years. What does one more night matter?" He walked quickly out of the circle of light, and Carly had a powerful urge to throw something hard and fierce.

Instead, she sat in the dirt and Jack, predictably, plopped down next to her.

She must have some secret masochistic streak in her, Carly decided, otherwise she wouldn't find herself in these miserable straits. She was terrified to give in to the rocket ship of need that had been fueling inside her all day, and even more scared that she might regret it for the rest of her lonely life if she didn't.

Without knowing it, Chase held in his hands a tantalizing promise, as golden as August wheat and yet as dark as a moonless winter night. What would she be willing to risk for a rare chance to dance for a while amid the fires of paradise, to hold back the cold, harsh light of day while tangled in the heat of his body? Her pride? Her self-esteem? Her brother's memory?

"What should I do, Jackson?" she moaned to the dog, who whined at the angst in her voice and laid his head in her lap. A nubby tongue licked her hand, and Carly obediently petted the dog. "At least you love me, don't you, sweetie?" Heaven knew, Chase didn't, she thought glumly. Sure, he might be attracted to her, but deep down she didn't doubt that she'd always be little Snarly Carly to him, with spiders in her hair and frogs in her pockets.

Why should it matter if a man like Chase Samuelson

cares about you or not? a mean little voice whispered. *He's the enemy, remember?*

He came back just then, water droplets clinging to his mustache and dripping from his battered baseball cap, and somehow, the words had a hollow ring to them. Instead of the fierce antipathy she tried to summon, all that answered her call was a sweet, familiar affection.

He looked tired, she suddenly realized, rising to her feet. Beyond tired, more like bone-deep exhausted. The fine crow's feet fanning out at the corners of his eyes looked deeper than they had earlier in the day. It was only when he bent to drop several saddlebags and an armload of firewood that she noticed the tight lines of pain around his mouth, and the way he winced when he straightened.

"You are an idiot, Chase Samuelson." She stood nose-to-nose with him, enunciating each word carefully while wishing she were bigger so she could knock some sense into him.

"But a hell of a good kisser. Or so I'm told."

She muttered a few more colorful phrases. "Here's the plan. I'm going to start a fire and warm up a can of something, while you use your head for something besides a windbreak—for a change—and give those knees a rest."

"I'm the guide, you're the client. It's my job to take care of you." He even managed a fairly credible leer, despite the pain she now recognized shadowing his face. "Just say the word, sweetheart, and I'd be willing to work at meeting *all* your needs."

"If you don't get off your feet, the only need of mine

you're going to meet is my overwhelming compulsion to punch something. Namely you."

"Does that mean if I do get off my feet, you'll let me satisfy a few of your, uh, other desires?" he asked hopefully.

"Sure," she responded, keeping her tone light despite the heat spreading through her at the images his words provoked. "But you'll have to catch me first, and in your present condition I'm pretty sure I could outrun you without even working up a sweat."

He grumbled a little more but finally hunkered down against the piled-up sleeping bags and camping pads. With his left leg extended and his forearms resting on the other bent knee, he watched her out of weary eyes while she laid the fire.

It didn't take long for the wood to ignite, and she soon had a snapping blaze to lend light and warmth to the cave. But by the time she found some canned stew and a can opener in their gear, Chase's eyes were closed and his even breathing told her he wasn't going to be eating anytime soon.

She watched him sleeping for a few minutes, the can opener forgotten in her hands. His head rested on the mound of bedding, and disgustingly long lashes fanned his cheeks. He gave a half smile in his sleep, and Carly found herself staring in fascination when one dimple appeared then disappeared again.

A comfortable emotion bubbled up in her chest, flowing through her limbs like the cleansing rain outside their sanctuary. It took her several seconds to recognize it. Tenderness. Strong and steady, slow and sweet. She wanted to hold him to her, to wipe away his pain, to share with him her own.

This was it, then, evidence of the love she thought he'd killed. It had been there all along, only hibernating until she let his warmth draw her back to life.

She loved Chase Samuelson. Had probably never stopped.

Carly hugged her arms, unable to look away from him. How could she have ever been stupid enough to actually believe she hated him?

She managed to extricate one of the sleeping bags from behind him without disturbing more out of him than an unconscious grumble. She unzipped it, and with hands that only trembled slightly, she spread it over him, tucking the sides in as carefully as a mother would with her sleeping, rumpled boy.

That wayward dimple made an appearance again as he snuggled into the comfort she'd provided, and Carly took a long, slow breath, slumping into a heap by the fire.

"Oh, Chase," she whispered. "What am I going to do with you?"

SEVEN

Sometime during the night, long after Carly had abandoned any attempts to stay warm by the dying fire and had snuggled as close to Chase as her pride and her own sleeping bag would allow, she awakened, disoriented. She tried to brush away the blankets of sleep, to discern what had disturbed her.

That sound, there it was again. A half-smothered moan, the eerie cry of someone in pain.

She came fully awake then, alarm pouring through her. Chase had always been stoic when he was hurting. When they were kids, he'd broken his arm while sledding with her family on the hill behind town hall. She remembered thinking he must be the bravest boy alive. Not once had he cried or even changed expressions to show the injury hurt. In fact, he'd teased her all the way to Doc Miller's office, while she wailed and carried on as if it had been her own arm.

She couldn't even comprehend the depth of pain it must take to make him moan like this. Scrambling up, she lit the kerosene lantern they'd brought. In the pale circle of light she could see he had kicked off the sleeping bag she'd covered him with. She could also see that his left knee looked unnatural, even through his jeans, with the heavy material bulging oddly in comparison with the right knee.

Her gasp awakened him. He sat up, instantly alert.

"What's wrong?"

"Oh, Chase," she whispered. "How could you let it go this long? We've got to get you out of those jeans. Now."

"Why, Miss Jacobs," he drawled, running a hand through his tousled hair. "I do declare, you're gonna make me blush."

She frowned. "And you're gonna make me get nasty and sic Jackson on you if you don't shuck your britches before that knee swells right through the seams."

He must have realized she was right. Without a shred of modesty, he unbuttoned the jeans and slid them over his hips, revealing navy blue underwear and muscled, hair-roughened legs.

Cheeks flaming, Carly shifted her gaze from that tempting flesh to his face. She caught a glimpse of disgust and what looked like self-contempt as he studied the angry red injury, but then their eyes met and an entirely different emotion sparked to life. It quivered between them as their gazes locked—awareness, then desire, then a burning, urgent need. Carly felt a tremor begin in her stomach and expand in concentric waves, like a rock made when thrown into a glassy mountain lake.

She drew in a shaky breath. "I'm, ah, going to get

some snow to pack on that. Maybe we can get the swelling down so you can move again."

She shoved on her boots without tying the laces, then grabbed a pan from the supplies and hurried out of the cave. The thunderstorm had blown away, leaving the air crisp and clean. It must be after midnight, she figured. The full moon of the night before had a chip out of one edge but still shone brightly enough for her to find a patch of leftover snow, sheltered by rocks from the scorching fingers of the sun.

She scooped it with her bare hands, not even noticing when they became numb from the cold. The heat from Chase's eyes still burned through her skin. This was absolutely insane, she thought. The man just had to look at her and she became as weak-kneed as a newborn foal.

She sat back on her heels when the pan was full, staring at the welcoming light spilling from the cave opening.

You can do this, she told herself. *You can go back into that cave where a lean, beautiful, half-naked male with a world of promise in his eyes waits for you.*

Just tend to his hurts, just pretend this sizzling force between you doesn't exist.

It's all a matter of willpower.

An image of him sprawled out on the sleeping bag, rumpled and sexy, flashed through her mind, and Carly groaned. The smack of her freezing hands over her face did absolutely nothing to cool her fevered imagination.

Who the Sam Hill was she kidding? She had about as much willpower when it came to Chase Samuelson as her mother did at a Sears white sale.

Sighing deeply, she squared her shoulders, picked up the snow-filled pan, and trudged back toward that beckoning light with all the enthusiasm of a turkey who'd just been invited to dine with the Pilgrims.

Chase had tossed some fresh wood on the fire. The little blaze burned brighter, the temperature in the cave already a few notches higher. He'd also straightened his sleeping bag and now sat on it, his left leg extended, totally uncaring that he was clad only in briefs and a shirt with the sleeves rolled up.

He was drinking from one of the containers of bottled water they'd brought along, and Carly froze in the cave opening. She couldn't move, hypnotized by the sight of him tipping the plastic bottle in the air. She saw his eyes close, his mouth tight around the narrow neck of the container. Saw the movements of his throat as he swallowed. Imagined the cool water sliding down that long length.

Still oblivious to her presence, he dragged his bare forearm across his mouth slowly, moistening the dark hair on his arm so it glistened in the firelight.

Carly swallowed hard, then shook her head angrily. Life simply wasn't fair. How was she supposed to fight his effect on her when he could turn the simple act of drinking into a sensual celebration?

Without stopping to think, she strode over to him and upended the snow-filled pan onto his leg. He stiffened but didn't jump, and guilt immediately washed over her. The man was in pain, for crying out loud.

Besides, it would have done more good if she'd poured it over her own head.

"Sorry," she said. "It slipped out of my hands."

He cocked his head. "I'm sure it did."

Battling valiantly to ignore the broad expanse of skin so tantalizingly close, she knelt on the sleeping bag next to him and began scooping the snow back into the pan. "It . . . probably would be best if I wrapped this in a towel, then you can pack it around your knee."

With the fire popping and dancing in the background, he leaned forward to help her, and they worked silently for a few minutes. Inevitably, it seemed, their hands collided as the last flakes of snow trickled into the pan, and he instinctively gripped hers, the rough pads of his thumbs rubbing against her palms. A shiver of awareness rippled through her, and Carly jerked her hands back and scrambled away, using her search for a towel as an excuse to try to regain both her breath and her equilibrium.

Maybe if she didn't look at him, she thought, if she could avoid those deep pools of blue that pulled at her like a riptide, she might be able to brush aside his impact on her. Her gaze on the task at hand, she packed the crusty snow into the towel.

It didn't help, she discovered. Even when she wasn't looking at him, Chase possessed a presence that filled every corner of the cave. He could be a mile away from her in the deepest, darkest hole in Wyoming and she knew she'd unerringly be able to find him.

The makeshift ice pack in hand, she knelt again on the sleeping bag.

"You don't have to do this," he said. "I've been through worse times. By sunup I'll be back to normal."

"Sure," she retorted, "if by 'normal' you mean so sore you can't walk a straight line."

"That's on a good day."

His disgruntled tone of voice drew her attention and she finally looked up. "You really live with this kind of pain all the time?"

"No." He took another swig from the water bottle, and her stomach clenched. "It comes and goes. It's worse right now because a few weeks ago I made the mistake of playing football with some of the older kids, and the little beasts all decided to tackle me at once. Me and my bad knees got hit by about four hundred pounds of attitude. My body hasn't quite forgiven me my stupidity yet."

Carly was about to ask him what kids he meant—it was the second or third time he'd referred to them—when she realized the tenor of his voice had changed, deepened.

She met his gaze and swallowed hard. Blatant desire blazed in his eyes, and she was suddenly conscious of her own attire—the same baggy flannel shirt he'd given her the night before unbuttoned over figure-hugging two-piece long johns.

It certainly wasn't the sexiest outfit she'd ever worn, but maybe he had some kind of weird thing for women in long underwear, she thought nervously. Heat flowed through her—glowing, yearning heat—and she curled her toes inside her hiking boots.

"What . . ." She cleared the huskiness out of her throat. "What do you usually do when you get in this condition?"

With one finger he tipped her chin up so she was again looking him in the eyes.

"Take a long, cold shower," he said solemnly, and then he kissed her.

Her eyes slid shut and her heart fluttered in her chest like a wild bird caught in a net. She gave one whimper against his mouth, disappointed in her own weakness, but her first taste of him—cinnamon and fire and man—turned the whimper into a throaty moan she couldn't stop. At the sound, Chase froze for an instant, his breath a whisper against her mouth, then he was caressing her with his lips, with his tongue. One hand snagged in her hair as he tilted her head so he could deepen the kiss, while the other brought her chest flush against his.

As kisses went, Carly thought dazedly, this one would knock the you-know-what out of the Richter scale.

She was melting in his arms like a piece of chocolate left out in the sun, and the knowledge frightened her. "Chase," she whispered, opening her eyes again, "I—I don't think this is such a great idea."

"Why not?" he whispered back. His fingers slid under her shirt, caressing bare skin, flirting dangerously close to the undersides of her breasts. "It feels pretty great to me."

She moaned and tilted her head back. "You . . . we're . . . I'm not . . ." The thoughts flitted around her head like elusive, dancing butterflies on a summer afternoon. She chased them, but they darted away too quickly.

He pressed a fleeting kiss to her neck. "You're not what?"

"Very good at this," she said weakly.

He trailed kisses over her cheek and back to her mouth, where their lips met and clung. A wild desire to taste him again, to absorb some of his essence, gripped her, and she flicked her tongue against his mouth. Like smoke and heaven, she thought. Delicious, beguiling, addicting. He deepened the kiss, his mouth firm and strong on hers, demanding things from her she'd never realized were hers to give.

This time it was he who pulled back, his eyes unfocused, his heart beating frenetically beneath her hand.

"I hate to disagree with you, sweetheart," he said, "but you're very *very* good at this."

He reached for her again, but her outstretched hand stopped him.

"I mean it, Chase." She fervently hoped she sounded more convincing to him than she did to herself. "We can't do this. You're . . . you don't have those kinds of feelings for me."

He snorted. "Honey, I've got so much feeling for you, I'm teetering on the edge of spontaneous combustion."

His arousal was pressing against her hip, but even without that evidence she could see his desire. It was in his eyes, the way he stared at her, sending skittery shivers across her skin. She saw tenderness and passion and something else she didn't recognize in his gaze. No man had ever looked at her that way. Not even close.

Was it only a momentary physical need that any woman could slake? The idea was like bile in her throat, and she quickly discarded it. He cared for her. She knew that, had known it, really, all along. If he desired her, too, could he grow to love her?

Did it matter? a tempting little voice asked her. Even if he didn't, at least she would have memories of this to take back to Cheyenne, to warm her when January winds piled mountains of snow against the door and everything was bleak and cold. Good memories to replace the bad. Sweet to replace the bitter. Love to replace the hate.

She turned back to him, wondering if she was about to make the biggest mistake of her life. The sight of him sitting there waiting, his eyes telling her he would stay away if she asked him to, sent all of her doubts flying away like Canada geese spooked by a shotgun blast.

Smiling shyly, she reached for the hand he held out to her. He yanked her into an embrace that stole her breath. His mouth met hers in a cataclysmic explosion, his hands buried in her hair. She met him kiss for kiss, loving the soft brush of his mustache, gasping when his tongue found its way to hers and licked and teased. By the time he pulled away, their mingled breathing echoed loudly in the cave.

Twining her hands around his neck, she pulled him back down to her. She couldn't get enough of him. She couldn't touch him enough, couldn't taste him enough.

While his kisses distracted her, he pulled the flannel shirt down off her shoulders. She let him slide it off her arms, and gasped when his hands slipped up under her top to caress her bare skin.

It wasn't enough. She wanted—no, she needed—to feel skin on skin. Her hands shaking, she moved away from him and pulled her top over her head. If she didn't do it now, she knew she'd never have the nerve.

She thought she'd be uncomfortable, being so exposed, so vulnerable, to him, but his words stopped her from snatching the shirt back to cover her breasts.

"Carly. Sweet Carly. You're the most beautiful thing I've ever seen." It sounded like a line, but one look at his face told her it wasn't. The stunned awe in his expression did more than anything else could have to put her at ease.

She moved back into his arms, loving the feel of his hard, hair-roughened chest against her skin. She rubbed against him, and her nipples hardened at the contact. With a groan, he grabbed her face in his big hands and covered her lips with his. "Much more of that, and I'm not going to last two seconds," he muttered against her mouth.

He lowered her to their sleeping bags, his weight shifted away from his injured knee. For a long moment, he stared at her in the firelight, his eyes glittering like a mountain lake in the sun.

"You're perfect," he whispered. "Absolutely perfect."

She wasn't. She was too small, too scrawny. "Sorry I don't exactly have prize-winnin' beefsteak tomatoes," she said, straining for humor.

A dimple appeared at one corner of his mouth. "I outgrew my taste for beefsteaks years ago. Give me the sweetness of a couple of ripe, plump cherry tomatoes any day."

She punched him in mock outrage. "Cherry tomatoes?" She never would have expected this sweet laughter, this happiness that bubbled out of her until she felt she could scoop it up and hold it in her hands.

"I mean it. You're perfect." All teasing was gone

from his voice, and his expression was serious as he dipped his head to whisper a gentle, closed-mouth kiss to the tip of the first breast, then the other.

The breath left her lungs as a torrent of sensation rushed through her, liquid heat pooling between her thighs. When he kissed her breasts again, this time laving them with his tongue, she gripped the sleeping bag, unable to move, to think, to do anything but float along in the waves of pleasure.

He must have spent hours kissing her, tasting her. They seemed suspended in time, hanging in a hazy, ethereal place filled with warmth and light, a place Carly never wanted to leave. She managed to unclench her fingers from the sleeping bag and move them to his hair, burying her hands in its luxurious silk.

A restless ache stole over her and her hips began an ancient, timeless rhythm, searching for something she couldn't name. The long johns she wore—the soft cotton ones she'd always thought were the most comfortable thing she owned—suddenly seemed painfully rough against her legs. So she felt vast relief, not awkward shyness, when Chase slid them off in one quick movement, leaving her only in panties.

"Smooth. Very smooth," she teased on a gasp.

He deliberately misunderstood and ran a hand down the length of her leg, from her thigh to her ankle and back, skimming over the heat of her essence hidden beneath her panties. "Yeah," he murmured, his mouth inches from hers while his hands explored. "Smooth as water gliding over stone. Smooth as satin and velvet. Smooth as a hawk soaring on a current of warm air."

Carly drew a ragged breath. His voice, gruff with

arousal, affected her soul as potently as his caresses. "Chase," she ordered weakly, "shut up and kiss me."

He laughed but still maintained that frustrating distance. "Bossy as ever, aren't we, little Carly?"

"Yes, we are." Annoyed at the familiar endearment, she crossed the minuscule space between them to take what he held so alluringly close. His low, sexy moan made her shiver even as she kissed him. Rolling to his back, Chase pulled her with him so she sprawled across him.

Now it was her turn to discover all the intriguing planes and hollows of his body, and she grabbed for the opportunity with both hands. While he watched with half-closed eyes, she stroked her fingers across his face, dipping into a dimple, tracing the shape of his lips.

Growing braver the longer her sensual exploration continued, Carly moved her hands to his chest, the light layer of crisp hair tickling her palms. She couldn't face the intensity that blazed from his eyes, so she closed her own, letting her hands say what she'd never dared. Fierce emotion rushed violently through her as she realized what she was doing. This sleek hardness, the seething, pulsing force beneath her fingertips, belonged to the man who owned her soul, whether he wanted to or not.

Never would she have believed she'd have the chance to be loving him like this, she thought, her hands skimming along his shoulders to feel the power in his arms. Fate had given her a rare and precious gift. Suddenly overwhelmed by it, she buried her face in his chest, but the feel of his warm skin—the taste of him, salty and vibrant—tantalized her so, she trailed her mouth across his chest until she found one hard nipple. She darted her tongue out, then bit gently, and was rewarded with a low moan from him and two tightly fisted hands clamping her in place.

"Did that hurt?" she asked.

"Pure agony," he growled. "Do it again."

"I aim to please," she murmured, moving to the other nipple and giving it the same attention he'd given her.

His hands pulled her up to meet his mouth, and after a long, deep kiss that robbed her of breath, he answered against her mouth, "You do please me, Carly Jane. You do."

Turning her onto her back once more, Chase kissed her again while his hands began a slow, circling journey to the center of her desire.

She gasped and cried his name when one long finger dipped inside her panties, into the core of her heat, drawing forth a shimmering, glittering rain. Suddenly panicking, as if she'd just lost a handhold on some steep cliff she was descending, Carly clamped her knees together. Patiently, he whispered kisses and words of passion against her mouth.

When he felt her relax, he shifted his hand, stroking his finger in and out in a rhythm older than the mountains that surrounded them.

Arching against him, her hips moving anxiously, restlessly, Carly felt a wild, pounding brilliance building. He slipped a second finger inside her while his thumb, with unerring accuracy, danced across the sensitive nub of flesh that guarded her secrets. Everywhere he touched, he left showering sparks of fire.

"That's it, sweetheart. Just let it go," he murmured

against her mouth, his fingers nestled tightly inside her. "Sweet, sweet Carly Jane. Burn for me."

His deep, throaty voice, urgent with need, loosed her last hold on control, and Carly tumbled over the edge, screaming his name as she convulsed around him.

He held her to him while she slowly regained her breath. "Chase," she finally whispered, "I didn't think I could . . . I never . . ." She couldn't find the right words, and avoided his eyes, suddenly embarrassed that she'd fallen apart like that. "Thank you," she mumbled at last.

"You do know how to humble a man," he said, resting his forehead against hers. "I want you so damn much, but I'm terrified I'll hurt you."

She smiled a little sadly. "You won't hurt me," she whispered back, wishing she believed her own words. He would hurt her. He wouldn't mean to, but she didn't doubt that in the end, he would leave her to go back to his own life and she would return to the cold world he'd briefly taken her from.

At least she would have this, she told herself. At least she would have this.

Tightening her arms around him, she reached up to kiss his corded neck. At the touch of her lips, a shudder rippled through him. He grasped her bottom and pulled her hips against his, against the heat she could feel scorching through two layers of cloth.

Quickly, without stopping to think, she shed her last wisp of clothing. He pulled off his briefs, and there was nothing left between them.

She longed to touch him as he'd touched her, but lingering shyness stilled her hands until he reached for her and guided her fingers to the heated length. Even with her few tentative touches, he was gasping her name and pulling back, breathing harshly. It gave her a heady sense of power that she could affect him like that. She reached for him again, only to have him stop her.

"Wait."

He shifted, then his hand was teasing the curls between her legs, until she opened for him. Before she knew what was happening, he was there, filling her, stretching her, engulfing her.

"Chase." Excitement built in her again, but he stayed buried inside her, unmoving, his weight all on one knee.

Only when her hands fluttered on his shoulders and her hips shoved gently against him did he groan and move within her. She arched against him, needing him, loving him.

"Chase . . . I . . ." Again, he swept away all conscious thought, everything but the heady, addicting feel of him nestled between her legs, of his long, even movements, of his lips showering kisses all over her face. Pressure pulsed deep within her, and she sought blindly for his lips. When their mouths and tongues met, she gasped his name again and felt the world explode in a thousand brilliant shards of light.

He stiffened above her as she spasmed around him, her name a prayer on his lips, then collapsed.

They lay that way for several minutes, Jackson's snoring and the fire's dying crackles the only sound in the cave besides their breathing. Then he was sliding off her and gathering her close, his hands tangled in her hair.

"You humble me, Carly," he repeated gruffly.

Suddenly exhausted, she snuggled into his warmth, drowsily kissed whatever expanse of skin was closest—his shoulder, it turned out—and fell asleep with a smile on her face.

"Jackson," Carly whispered. The hound's ears immediately perked up, and he lumbered to his feet. He loped after her as she quietly left the cave, stepping outside into the pale light of early morning. "We've got to go earn our paychecks, buddy."

She spared one more quick look at Chase. He slept peacefully, with the unzipped sleeping bag they'd shared rucked about his hips. Carly wanted to touch him, wanted to feel again the heat of that wide bare chest, but she knew if she did she'd be unable to stop herself from curling against his side again and sleeping the day away.

While the idea held enormous appeal, Carly needed some distance, some literal and emotional space between them so that she could try to put the events of the last twenty-four hours into perspective, try to regain the equilibrium he had swept away the previous night.

Using the directions the two hikers had given to Verl, it took her less than ten minutes to find the two bear carcasses. Or what was left of them, anyway.

She swallowed nausea as the thick, heavy stench of death filled her nostrils. The bears had probably been dead about a week, she figured, judging by the extent of the decomposition. The mangled piles of putrid flesh were barely recognizable as bear. Whatever damage the poachers had done to the animals had been compounded by the elements and hungry scavengers.

Carly sat back on her heels and closed her eyes for a moment. Anger and a deep frustration warred within her. It didn't matter how many fat-cat poachers she snared. Like a relentless tide of sludge, they continued to come, oozing into every wild spot in the country.

One might occasionally be put out of circulation, but hundreds more stood poised to take his place. It was like trying to chip away at the Wind Rivers with a pick and a shovel, she thought angrily. Like trying to drain a river with a leaky bucket.

Sighing wearily, she pulled out her camera and photographed the scene, walking carefully so she didn't inadvertently disturb the area. After two weeks of wet weather, she doubted she'd find any tracks, but even meticulously careful poachers always left behind some signature. After she'd shot the bears from every angle, she set the camera aside and began scouring the terrain, feeling her way on hands and knees through the pine needles and spongy wet leaves around the carcasses. She searched the whole clearing in expanding circles, before rising to her feet in disgust.

Nothing. Not a cigarette butt, not a frayed length of rope, not a footprint.

"What now?" she asked out loud.

Jackson gave an answering bark, and she noticed him sniffing around in a stand of trees a few hundred feet away. A spot, she realized, that would be perfect for lying in wait for a mama bear and her cub to come down to the water source. Any lingering weariness vanished in the thrill of the search, and after a few minutes of sifting carefully through dirt and leaves, she unearthed half a dozen shell casings. Probably a semiautomatic, she figured, just like the other poachings had been.

She started to stand when a flash of red caught her eye. Another shell casing, she thought, sweeping aside the leaves.

She was wrong. It wasn't a shell casing. Excitement coursed through her as with gloved fingers she extracted a muddy Swiss army knife from the springy ground cover and placed it in a plastic evidence bag.

It hadn't been there long, she figured. No rust marred the metal, and despite the mud, the red plastic case looked in pristine condition. Holding the bag in the air so she didn't inadvertently smudge any fragile fingerprints, Carly studied it with professional detachment.

Given her limited knowledge of Swiss army knives, she could tell this was a high-end model that probably had a dozen little attachments ranging from a can opener to scissors, even a tiny saw. She flipped the bag around, then felt her heartbeat quicken at what she saw on the other side—an inscription in gilt lettering that read, "Next time you'll be prepared. Love, J."

What a break! If her luck held, all she'd have to do to nab these poachers was a little intensive leg work back in Whiskey Creek to find out if any places around there sold this particular style and brand of knife. If she was really, really lucky, she would unearth a paper trail of special messages inscribed in the last year or so.

Of course the knife could be from some mail-order place, but she could easily check those out too. She had a hunch, though, that these poachers were strictly local. Bears weren't that common in this part of the country, not common enough that you could stumble across one without knowing exactly where to look. It wouldn't be cost-effective for some out-of-state operation to move into the area, not when places like Alaska and the Ozarks had a much higher concentration of bears.

Feeling better than she had all morning, she gathered the shell casings and the knife and tucked them carefully into her waist pack. She could go back to the camp now, but she hesitated, her thoughts on the man who waited for her there and the achingly sweet memories of the night they'd shared.

Embarrassment turned her face pink as she remembered her wild response to Chase, the way her cries of passion had echoed off the damp walls of the cave. She had never even imagined making love could be so sharp and intense, so visceral.

She wasn't exactly experienced, she admitted to herself. The only man she'd slept with was the one she'd nearly become engaged to, until she realized—the night before they were to buy a ring—that pleasing her mother was a sorry basis for a marriage. Phillip deserved a woman who loved him.

Perhaps even then she'd subconsciously known she still loved Chase. It frightened her though, her quicksilver response to him. She was suddenly both eager and afraid to return to camp. On the one hand, she longed to experience again the wild river of need he'd created in her; on the other, she was terrified she had dived in so far over her head, she'd never be able to swim to safety.

Her stomach grumbled, reminding her that dinner had been tepid soup and a few crackers. Chase probably had breakfast cooking now, she thought, and some of that incredible coffee of his.

When hot campfire coffee was involved, she could face just about anything. She grinned and whistled for Jackson, who bulleted past her at a full run toward camp.

"I could have used a little moral support here, buddy," she muttered to the already disappearing dog.

Magpies chattered angrily as she neared the cave, and Carly was greeted by the scent of bacon mingling with the sharp tang of pine and sage.

Thirty feet from their camp, she stopped short, a smile blooming across her face at the scene playing out in front of her. In the clearing near the cave, Chase sat on his haunches in front of Jackson, and the two members of the male species were giving each other unblinking stares.

"I guess you know we're going to have to make friends now," Chase said, and Jack's tail began a jerky rhythm. "I don't want to have to make her choose between us, because I reckon I'd be the one spending the night in the doghouse, if you catch my meaning."

Jackson barked and Chase chuckled. He reached out to scratch the dog's jowly chin, which sent the animal onto his back, his eyes closed in ecstasy. "Yeah, yeah. You know I'm right, don't you? It was nothing personal anyway, just pure small-minded jealousy. If I could have that woman look at me with half the emotion she wears when she sees your mangy face, I'd willingly endure any torture those doctors could dream up."

Delighted by his words, Carly started moving closer to the pair but stopped when Chase spoke again.

"We're both going to have to give a little if this is going to work. It's a two-way road here. I'll let you lick my face a few times if you tell me how you get that woman of yours to open up and give you a scratch or two."

She laughed out loud at the twin puzzled expressions they wore at the incomprehensibility of women.

"You just have to ask me real, real nice," she called out.

Chase looked up, not seeming a bit embarrassed to be caught carrying on such an intimate conversation with a dog. He smiled back at her, warm and welcoming, and that one smile shoved aside all her worries about how to deal with him this morning.

"Pretty, pretty, please," he said, "with strawberry swirl ice cream on top, can you give me a little scratch behind the ears?"

She smiled as she walked up to him, awed by the beauty of the morning and the sweetness of this big, muscled man.

"I'd be happy to, but somehow I don't think it's a scratch you really want, now is it, Chase?" Her voice sounded low and throaty in the high mountain air.

Instant desire kindled in his eyes, and he reached for her. "Now that you mention it, ma'am, it sure as hell isn't."

Being in his arms felt like walking into a warm kitchen after a long cold snap, she thought. She kissed him, her mouth meeting him taste for taste, her hands gripping his neck. All her fears faded, leaving only this vivid moment, the scratch of his stubbled face against her skin, his wet hair under her fingertips. He smelled divine, she thought, filling her senses with him. Pine soap and leather tack and male. The most erotic combination she could possibly imagine.

Another harsher smell invaded, and she drew back, sniffing the air.

"Uh, Chase, your bacon's burning."

"Tell me about it," he growled, cupping her bottom and pulling her hard against his arousal.

She gave a shaky gasp, then laughed huskily. "I meant the bacon you were fixing for breakfast."

He dropped his arms and looked at the camp stove, where thick plumes of acrid smoke were curling into the trees.

"That's what you get, missy, for being such an irresistible distraction." Moving quickly, he removed the frying pan from the stove and turned off the propane. "Not completely irresistible, apparently," she muttered, fighting a fierce urge to call him back into her arms.

He must have overheard, because he came back to her and tipped her face up, bestowing a gentle kiss to the tip of her nose. "Carly, honey, if I had my way, I'd carry you into that cave and make love to you all day and all night. All damn week, for that matter."

His words conjured up a heavenly picture that made her flush. It was exactly what she wanted, and her own need scared her silly. "I . . ." Her voice trailed off as she scrambled for words, and she knew her sudden panic was etched across her face.

"Don't knock me over with your enthusiasm here, sweetheart," he said wryly.

"Chase, I'm sorry. I'm just . . . I need a little time to get used to all this, okay? Just a little time."

His smile, both wistful and accepting, nearly had her flying back into his arms, despite her lingering fears.

"How hungry are you?" he asked.

Voracious, she thought. But not for food.

She shrugged. "Why?"

"If you can wait an hour or so, I could fry us up some brook trout for breakfast."

Her mouth instantly watered at the idea of fresh high country trout sautéed in lemon and butter, the way they'd all learned to fix it in his grandpa's dented frying pan on the banks of the Whiskey.

The look on her face gave him his answer. "Great," he said. "You just go ahead with your official business, and I'll see if I can convince a few big ones to flop onto our plates."

"My official business, at least this part of the investigation, is finished."

"Was it gruesome?"

She nodded tightly. "That's one word for it."

"Poor thing," he murmured, drawing her back into his arms, an unspoken offer of comfort. She clung to him for a moment, her cheek pressed to the brushed cotton of his gray shirt. She closed her eyes and rested there, content to lean against his strength for a moment.

She felt too fragile in his arms, Chase thought, as if she could be caught up by the next gust of wind and carried away like a dry leaf.

He felt profound amazement that she possessed such courage, such iron control. How did she have the sheer guts to relentlessly confront things she obviously had such a hard time with? Even now, he could feel her tremble every once in a while with delayed reaction.

It made him grateful that he hadn't rushed her into his arms and back into the cave, despite the desire that pulsed under his skin. There were too many undercurrents going on between them. Making love again before she had come to terms with their being lovers would only complicate things for her, and she didn't need complications right now.

She took a deep breath and pulled away, dry eyed, and his heart cracked a bit.

"Sorry to be such a baby," she said. "It just gets to me sometimes."

He would have embraced her again, but she stuck her hands in her back pockets and thrust her shoulders back, looking for all the world like the cocky tomboy she'd been.

"Hey, I'm starving," she said. "And those trout aren't going to wait all morning."

He smiled at her bravado. "You didn't sleep much last night. Why don't you take a little siesta while I catch breakfast?" He headed toward the gear.

"I . . . Chase . . ."

He turned. "Yeah?"

"Could I . . . come with you? Borrow the other rod, I mean, and go fishing with you?"

His smile widened, admiration and relief and a fierce love for her soaking through him. He reached for her hand. "You ought to know by now, Carly Jane Jacobs, that you never, ever have to ask me that."

EIGHT

Chase couldn't believe how content he felt. Even with his knees hurting like a sonuvabitch, he wished they weren't on their way out of the mountains.

It had been a close to perfect day. They'd fished until noon, eaten a late brunch of fish, and had been on the trail for the last six hours, warm sunshine their companion.

He wanted to stay at least one more day, and he freely admitted to himself why. He was afraid. Afraid that Carly would pull away from him again when they returned to the lowlands, that she would use the vortex of passion between them as another excuse to avoid him. Like some primeval man, he wanted to keep her there in the dank cave, selfishly hoarding the peace they'd found together.

But Carly wanted to keep moving while it was daylight, saying she was eager to return to Whiskey Creek and report whatever it was she'd found up there. If not for the way she spontaneously touched him whenever he rode close to her, or the way her face flushed when their eyes met, he would have thought she was anxious to get away from him.

Desire simmered between them, like a pulsing backbeat to the sweet harmony they'd begun to relearn together. Each time she smiled at him, he remembered with perfect clarity her flowing passion as she'd come apart in his arms.

He was in the middle of reliving it again when Rebel stumbled on a rock on the trail, jolting Chase in the saddle. To his shame, he couldn't stop a quick grimace of pain as his knee slammed against the horse's ribs with a hard thump.

It was just his bad luck that Carly happened to be looking back at that moment. "Okay," she said. "We'll stop here for the night."

"Not on my account, we won't," he returned sharply. Damn, he hated this weakness of his.

"Chase, you're a little old for these he-man endurance games, don't you think?"

Yeah, so what? he thought grumpily. Age has nothing to do with the purely male desire not to look like a big baby in front of his woman.

His woman? He sat up straighter in the saddle, the reins slack in his hand. Carly certainly wasn't anything of the sort, and she'd probably smack him for even entertaining such a chauvinistic idea. But he suddenly wanted her to be his woman, with a fierce, ancient hunger. Wanted to wake every morning of his life to her slow, sweet smile that changed a woman of simple beauty into someone rare and precious, to watch her grow older, to watch their children . . .

"Chase?"

He blinked, realizing he'd been staring at her. "Sorry. What did you say?"

"I said, we're stopping here. I don't want to argue with you about this, okay?"

She was trying so hard to look stern and uncompromising that he couldn't help laughing.

"Fine, boss lady, whatever you say." He scanned the area, trying to gain his bearings so he could find them a good place to camp, then grinned. He'd been so busy fantasizing he hadn't realized their location. It was one of his favorite places to camp on this trail, for reasons he couldn't wait to show to Carly.

Following one of the hundreds of nameless streams in the Wind Rivers, he led them to a clearing sheltered from the ever-present wind by big spruce and quaking aspen. They worked together efficiently making camp. While Chase curried the horses and hobbled them in a wide meadow plump with young grass, Carly set up both tents, selected water-smoothed rocks from the creek to create a fire ring, and gathered plenty of wood. When she was finished, she perched on one of the folding camp chairs and made notes in a spiral-bound blue notebook, nibbling occasionally on the sandwich he'd made for her.

Chase couldn't stop looking at her. With her hair falling out of the braid and her nose pinkened by the sun, she looked so vibrant and alive that he wondered if he wouldn't scorch his fingers if he touched her.

He had to stop watching her like some googly-eyed junior-high kid, he thought. He turned back to the fire he was building and was about to strike a match when he saw her stretch gingerly, her hands rubbing the small of her back. The fire could wait until they returned, he decided. It was time to show her why he loved camping here.

"Are you at a place where you can stop for a while?" he asked.

She looked up, her gaze slightly unfocused like a half-blind baby kitten. "Sure. Why?"

"I want you to see something, but we might be away from camp for an hour or so."

"Sounds great. I could use a walk after sitting on a horse all day." She stood up, stretching her arms above her head, and his body tightened at the feline sensualness of the movement.

"Yeah, so could I," he muttered, willing away his uncomfortable arousal. "Bring a change of clothes."

She looked askance at the towels he gathered and the little bottle of Camp Suds, a biodegradable soap used for everything from washing dishes to washing hair. "You are absolutely up in the night if you think I'm taking a dip in any high mountain stream."

He grinned. "Trust me, sweetheart."

"I believe that's exactly what Clyde said to Bonnie, just before he handed her a machine gun."

"Come on, Carly, I dare you," he taunted. "Grab some clean clothes and come with me."

She sent him a look of blatant distrust, then slipped inside her tent. She returned a few minutes later with a little bundle.

"Lead on, O mighty scout."

They walked along the stream, following a narrow animal trail through thick brush for several minutes before veering sharply uphill. Not far off the path was a geothermal spring that fed into a shallow twenty-foot wide bowl before flowing into the creek. Steam drifted into the air while little carbon dioxide bubbles popped and fizzed all across the natural hot tub's surface.

Chase dipped a hand in to test the water and found it perfect—warm enough to suck away the pain, but not hot enough to scald.

"Chase, this is incredible! How did you ever find it, tucked away up here?"

Desire shot through him at the pleasure in her voice, and he staunchly tamped it down. He didn't bring her here to seduce her. He planned to give her all the time she needed to come to grips with the feelings blooming between them.

He couldn't risk looking at her, though, not when he was teetering on the edge of control like this. Forcing his attention to finding a dry spot for the towels, he answered her. "A few years ago I brought some of my buddies from the team up this way for fishing. One night a couple of our horses broke their hobbles. We had to track them for a while and we stumbled on this place."

He finally looked at her and felt the blood rush away from his brain at the sight of her stripping down to her underclothes. She slid into the water, all bare limbs and blissful expression. He stiffened as she gave a low, completely sybaritic moan of ecstasy at the healing, caressing touch of the water.

"Yeah, well, uh, you go on ahead and soak all you want," he stammered. "I'll, um, just wait down the trail a ways so you can have some privacy."

He'd only gone a few feet when her voice, throaty and warm, drifted across the water. "Chase. Don't be an idiot. There's plenty of hot water for everybody, especially a bull-headed ex-jock in a lot more pain than he'll ever admit. Besides, after last night, I'd say we don't have too many secrets left between us, do we?"

He winced. That was just it. It was those last few secrets he was afraid of.

Chase, old buddy, this was a stupid idea, he berated himself. He wanted her so ferociously, his entire body throbbed with need, and not just the parts he would normally expect to be whistling Dixie. He felt it clear down to the soles of his feet, in the tips of his fingers, in every blasted hair follicle. It was as if he'd touched a live wire just long enough for a quick blast of power to leave every cell humming.

He stripped off his shirt and unbuttoned his jeans, sliding them over his hips. They were halfway down his thighs before he realized his boots were still on. Fortunately, Carly was floating on the other side of the bowl and couldn't see him making a fool of himself. What was it about her that turned him into such a fumbling, awkward boy?

Still, the water did feel terrific. Almost as soon as he slid into it, the pain in his knees abated. It was the most comfortable he'd been the entire trip—except when he was bathing his fingers in her sweet fire, he thought, then regretted it when the memory once again stirred his body to life.

Some of the minerals in the water had hardened over eons of time, depositing themselves around the edge of the pool to form a smooth bench. Chase settled onto it and leaned his head against the bank, letting the soothing heat relax him.

He was enormously grateful for the murky water that concealed the evidence of his desire. He'd promised to give her time, and he tried to be a man who kept his promises. He didn't want to pressure her into anything she might resent or regret later.

All his grand convictions just about disintegrated into nothing when he opened one eye to find Carly working on her braid, tugging on it until her hair frothed to her shoulders and around her face in a gold-tinged cloud of glory.

Oh, hell.

He struggled valiantly to fill his mind with pure thoughts. Motherhood. Apple pie. Baseball.

"Hey, scout. Where's that soap you brought?"

He swallowed hard. "Uh, by the clothes."

"Would you mind bringing it over here?"

Would you mind having a little mercy on a man? he thought, blindly reaching for the Camp Suds. With a sense of inevitability, he made his way through the waist-deep water to where Carly floated blissfully, only her face resting above the water.

She opened her eyes, and he tried to shunt away the naked longing on his face. Carly just smiled, a secretive woman's smile that was like a fist in his gut. She knew exactly what she was doing to him, the little brat, he realized.

Without thinking beyond his first impulse to pay her back for torturing him, he moved behind her and sat on the mineral ledge. He pulled her onto his lap, her back to him.

"Chase, what do you think you're doing?"

"Relax, darlin'. I'm just gonna wash your hair."

He grinned at the audible gulp she made. She didn't pull away, though, so he poured a bit of the concentrated soap into his hands and worked it into the wavy hair. He took his time with it, too, rubbing her scalp over and over with his fingers, pulling his hands through the soft curls.

All too soon, he realized that instead of alleviating his tension, he'd only exacerbated it. And then some. The feel of her smooth legs drifting against his, of her hair rippling over his fingers, and most especially of her bottom resting snugly against his arousal was driving him beyond any hope of self-control.

"Time to rinse," he muttered, standing up so abruptly she splashed into the water. He grabbed her before her head went under and set her on her feet, then dived for the other side of the pool.

With superhuman effort, he managed to at least get his breathing under control by the time she was done washing the soap from her hair.

She'd asked for time, and he'd give it to her, by damn, even if it killed him. Which it very likely might. Chase knew he should probably climb right out and get his butt back to camp. Trouble was, he'd left the bottle of Camp Suds on the bank where he'd washed her hair and he had three days of trail dust he was itching to shed.

Carly must have caught his gaze as he studied the bottle, trying to figure out how he could get it without coming close to her. She smiled and grabbed it, then waded through the water toward him.

No, Carly, he begged silently, that sense of inevitability returning. *Don't do this. I promised.*

"Your turn," she said.

"Just give me the soap. Believe me, it would be better for both of us if I washed my own hair. Thanks all the same."

"Un-uh." She held the bottle away.

He didn't dare reach for it. If he missed and touched any of that delectable skin of hers, he'd never be able to let her go. Fighting for control, he stood as still as possible as she moved behind him and climbed onto the ledge. The added height put his head level with her chest.

He took a deep, shaky breath, closing his eyes as she worked the lather into his hair. Coupled with the languorous spell the warm water cast over him, he had to struggle to stay on his feet.

He shuddered when her slick, soapy hands slid to his shoulders, leaving tremors of awareness along their way. Aware of the very real risk he might turn and plunge himself into her, regardless of any promise, he endured while she soaped his back and his forearms. When she slipped her hands beneath his arms to reach his chest, her breasts scorching his back through her thin, wet bra, he felt as if he'd turned to rock, just like the mineral deposits beneath his feet.

He could have withstood even that—oh, he might have popped a few blood vessels along the way, but he would have survived. Yet when she trailed wet fingers across his stomach and dipped into his briefs, he jerked away, swimming to the other side of the pool as if his toe had just encountered a piranha, leaving a trail of suds in his wake.

"What's the matter?" Carly asked when he surfaced and faced her.

"You wanted time, dammit," he said fiercely. "And I promised to give it to you. Don't play these teasing little games with me unless you want the hourglass to run out of sand in about three seconds."

That secretive smile lifted her mouth; her eyes gleamed a blatant invitation. "Oops. There goes the last grain. Guess my time's up."

Chase froze, trying to clamp down his elation. "You better know exactly what you're doing, sweetheart. The minute I touch you, I'm not letting go until morning. If even then."

"Promises, promises." The teasing words were barely out of her mouth before he was diving through the water.

She met him halfway, in the pool's center, and her arms encircled him so tightly it stole his breath.

"What took you so long, scout?" she murmured against his chest.

He growled, tugging her hair back so he could reach her mouth. She melted into him deliciously, eagerly, and by the time he lifted his head for air, they were both breathing hard.

"You taste so good," she whispered. "I always wondered what your kisses would be like."

In his present condition, the idea of her wondering about such a thing was almost more than he could handle. "What did you discover?" he asked.

"You taste like cinnamon candy. Cinnamon and pine and heaven."

He'd thought he couldn't want her more than he already did.

He was dead wrong.

Closing his eyes, Chase leaned his forehead against hers. "You sure do know how to sweet-talk a man, Carly Jane Jacobs."

Her smile tickled his mouth. "I haven't even started sweet-talking you yet. That's just my warm-up. I could go on for hours on your dimples alone."

"I don't have dimples," he growled. "They're just tiny indentations you can barely see."

She laughed. "Whatever you say, Chase."

"I say you better watch your smart mouth, darlin', if you don't want to find it full of mineral water."

"For some strange reason, threats lose something coming from a man with sweet dimples like those."

Chase shook his head sadly. "Don't say I didn't warn you." He released her and reached under the water to push her off balance. She splashed backward and went under, then gained a foothold and came up sputtering and laughing.

"You are mean and spiteful, Chase Samuelson, and I'm going to tell your grandpop on you." She aimed a mock glare at him while she wiped the water from her face.

"I'll just tell him you started it," he returned, then taking pity on her, he grabbed a towel from the bank and waded over to her.

"Here, let me do that for you." He awkwardly wiped the water from her face and neck. Just as he began patting her hair to keep it from dripping water back into her eyes, she went on the offensive, standing on tiptoe to kiss him.

The playful mood shifted swiftly back to passion. Chase captured in his mouth the sexy little moan she made and barely managed to stay upright when she pressed against him, only three skimpy pieces of cloth separating his hardness and her sweet softness.

Awash in the magic of her, he never suspected treachery was afoot. He vaguely registered she was maneuvering him backward, but just assumed she wanted to be closer to the edge. Only when he felt the ridge in the pool's floor where it rose did he realize what she was doing. By then, it was too late. Off-balance from the shifting level and her weight pressing against him, he could do nothing except grab her and pull her under with him, their lips still meshed together, their limbs entangled.

Warm bubbles popped against their skin as the water covered them, but Chase didn't let go of her. She hugged him back tightly, her mouth opening for him.

Only after he'd used the water as a veil to relieve them both of their last bits of clothing did he pull them up for air.

He stood there gasping, shuddering with a need more powerful than the mighty powers of the earth that seethed and boiled beneath them, creating this wondrous place.

Somehow he summoned the strength of will to speak. "This is your last chance. Are you absolutely sure this is what you want?"

"In all my twenty-seven years," she answered solemnly, "I've never been more sure of anything."

He closed his eyes, awed once again by the marvelous gift he'd been given, then he lifted her in his arms and carried her to the edge of the pool. He laid her gently on the soft grassy bank, then covered her with his body.

She held him tight, pressing darting kisses on his neck, his chin, anywhere her mouth could reach. Those kisses were driving him crazy, and it didn't help when her hips began to rock restlessly beneath him.

Volcanic heat blasted him when he traced his fingers from her face to one pouting breast, and she pressed against him at the contact. Encouraged, he dipped his head until his mouth found the pebbly peak, and he rolled it between his tongue and his teeth, around and around, back and forth. Her breath came in little gasps, and she dug her hands into his hair, clamping him to her.

"You're so damn sweet," he muttered against her skin, then shifted his attention to her other breast while his hand began an inexorable descent to the source of her inner fire. When he touched her, thrusting one finger high inside, he felt his breath catch as she arched against him wildly, gasping his name.

The feel of her lava flow of desire—for him, only for him—nearly snatched all coherent thought from his head. "I can't wait," he said. "I'm sorry."

"Who asked you to wait?"

With one powerful stroke, he sheathed himself in her heat, savoring every tremor of her flesh surrounding him. If he did this ten times a day for the rest of his life, he thought, he would never tire of her.

Her legs locked around him as he drove into her.

Supporting himself on one knee and one arm, he reached the other hand between them, finding the nub of her desire. He stroked it gently in a heady contrast as he pounded into her.

He felt the spasms of her completion begin deep inside her, then she arched against him one last time. The sound of her crying his name echoed in the pines around them as he threw his head back, pouring his fulfillment into her.

As conscious thought seeped back into him, a fierce desire to tell Carly how he felt about her seized Chase. But he sensed she wasn't ready to hear the words, that she would withdraw from him. Instead, he pulled her into his arms and slid back into the healing water. He sat on the mineral bench and held her on his lap, stroking her satin skin, whispering sweet words.

Carly floated along in the water, hardly believing she was here, in Chase's arms. She'd thought making love with him the night before was an unbelievable experience. This, though, was beyond anything she'd ever dared imagine.

"You have no idea how many times I've dreamed of having you here like this." His voice was a rough caress against her ear.

She shivered, then jerked her head around to stare at him as his words registered. "Me? You dreamed about me? Doing *this*?"

He quirked a half smile. "Relentlessly. And I must say, the fantasy compares to the reality about like a pleasant spring breeze compares to a whirling tornado."

"You're talking about since I've been home, right?"

"Since about the time you turned fifteen, sweetheart.

I thought I was some dirty old man. Here I was a nineteen-year-old college student having all kinds of wild ideas about a mouthy teenager I'd known since she was barely out of diapers."

For a minute, she could do nothing but stare at him, speechless. How could he possibly have been attracted to her back then, when she'd been nothing but a smart aleck kid with a bad attitude? He'd never, for one second, given her any clue of it. He'd treated her exactly as Mike had done, with brotherly teasing and amused affection.

"But you've never . . . You didn't . . ."

"What? Act on it? Hell, Carly, you were only fifteen years old! I was practically a grown man. A man who knew good and well he had no business entertaining those sorts of thoughts about his best friend's little sister. And when you finally started growing up, you wouldn't let me within three miles of you."

He must be remembering things wrong, she told herself. He'd dated every girl in the whole county, for crying out loud. She knew, because she'd been ready to spit nails every time he'd gone out with a new one. True, he'd never shown more than passing interest in any of them until . . . until . . .

"What about Jessie?" The question was yanked from her, and instantly his expression became as closed as Whiskey Creek on a Sunday.

"Jessie didn't have anything to do with the way I felt about you."

Apparently not, she thought, a bitter taste on her tongue. Whatever hormonal aberration he'd felt for her so long ago apparently hadn't been very strong. Otherwise he wouldn't have moved in on his best friend's girl.

Carly tried to scramble away from him, suddenly needing to put space between them, but his arms tightened implacably around her. "Carly, stop it," he said, as she struggled to free herself. "Listen to me. For once, will you just stop running away from me?"

All the energy left her, and she sagged in his arms.

"We all made mistakes that spring," he said quietly, "mistakes that had some pretty horrible consequences. There's nothing I can do about those. I've wished hundreds of times, hell, probably hundreds of thousands of times, that I'd handled things differently. The past is gone, though. Mike's gone, and no matter how badly we might want to change it, you know as well as I do that we can't. The only thing we *can* change is how we deal with it. Do we learn from it, or do we let it control every waking moment of the rest of our lives, let it eat away at anything good until all we have left is a fistful of nothing?"

"I miss him, Chase." The anguished plea was as close as she'd come to crying in years. She felt his lips brush across her hair, and his arms again tightened around her. Instead of feeling constricting, now they gave comfort, and she let herself lean into him.

"I miss him too, sweetheart." He pulled her onto his lap. "I miss him too."

They stayed that way for a long time, not speaking. Carly didn't think she would ever feel as close to another human being as she did then, wrapped in Chase's arms in that healing water while the sun slid behind the mountains.

A strange feeling swept through her, so unfamiliar that it took her several long moments to recognize it. Peace. She was completely, totally at peace for the first time in years. She smiled to herself and nestled closer to Chase's warmth.

When the night began to grow colder, they dressed and walked hand in hand to the tents. He unzipped hers for her and stood silently by while she climbed inside.

"Get some sleep," he said. "With any luck, tomorrow night you'll be in a nice, comfortable bed."

He turned to go, and she realized she couldn't bear the thought of leaving the mountains, of leaving this sweetness behind. "Chase, stay. Please?"

He smiled, a slow, tender smile that took her breath. "Sure, boss lady. Whatever you say."

She slept with a smile on her face and his arms around her.

It didn't last.

The next morning dawned clear and beautiful. Carly awakened to find herself alone in the tent, only a glowing ache between her thighs and the pine and leather scent of Chase on her skin to remind her of the night they'd shared. They'd made love—what was it?—three, four times? She'd lost count, but each time she felt him tighten his hold on her heart.

Hard truths were always difficult to face at seven o'clock in the morning, but she forced herself to face this one anyway. She was completely, undeniably, irreversibly in love with Chase Samuelson. This was no hero-worship, either, of a girl pining over her big brother's best friend, but the full, strong, true love of a woman.

The snick of the tent flap being unzipped startled her, and a second later Chase's dark unshaved face peeked through the opening. When he saw she was awake, he reached in and kissed her, a juicy, sumptuous, immensely satisfied smack on the lips.

He always had been a morning person, she thought, slightly disgruntled as he chased away the last few vestiges of sleep.

"Mornin'," he said. "I've got breakfast waiting when you're decent."

"When I'm decent?" She faked outrage. "What are you implying, Samuelson? That I'm some kind of shameless hussy who took advantage of your meek nature and had her way with you?"

He laughed. "Let me rephrase that, considering that I can't imagine anything more decent than you are right now." He drew a rough thumb over the tip of one breast. "When you are dressed, hiding all this luscious temptation from my meek nature, breakfast is waiting for you. And so am I, lazybones."

She shivered as he withdrew his hand and slid his head out of the tent. It felt so good to laugh again, she thought.

Fifteen minutes later—and fully dressed—she returned from washing up at the creek to find Chase throwing a stick for Jackson to catch.

"My poor dog doesn't know what he's getting into, playing catch with a man whose throwing arm used to be legendary."

"Used to be? *Used to be?*" he exclaimed, even as his mouth turned up at the edges.

"Sorry. Whose arm is *still* legendary. Is that better?"

"Much." Crossing to the fire, he poured her coffee, then delivered it with a smile and a kiss.

For a moment, she actually forgot his delectable brew in the wonder of his mouth on hers. He stepped back just as the hot mug began burning her fingers.

"Sit down and relax for a minute," he said. "The batter's ready. I just need to pop the frying pan on the camp stove."

Pancakes and coffee in the mountains, she thought. And Chase, of course. Life suddenly seemed amazingly rich. Her heart overflowing, Carly slipped into one of the camp chairs and watched him cook while she sipped the steaming coffee.

He moved with a quick, efficient grace, his arm muscles barely stretching as he flipped the pancakes with a flourish. When he smiled at her, she remembered how he'd looked bending over her, his face flushed with passion and tenderness while he drew her down into the soft grass beside the mineral spring.

"Too bad we don't have time to make another trip to the swimming hole."

She started at his words, sloshing coffee out of the mug and onto her shirt.

"Blast it," she muttered, and unzipped the duffel she'd carried her things in when she washed up. Her hands fumbled past the evidence bag with the Swiss army knife in it before she found some tissues to wipe up the mess.

Chase handed her a plate brimming with fluffy, fruit-topped pancakes. "Mmmm. Heavenly," she said after she'd tasted the first forkful. "I could really get used to this, to you taking care of me." She smiled at him until she realized how her words could be construed. Ducking her head, she felt hot color spread from her neck to the roots of her hair.

The last thing she wanted was for him to feel pressured. He'd never said anything about what would happen when they left the mountains. Maybe he wouldn't want to continue this fragile relationship when they headed back to the lowlands. She hadn't exactly made it easy on him.

"I'd like that." His words were quiet in the cool morning air. His gaze, solemn and direct, never wavered from hers.

"Like—like what?" she asked weakly.

"Taking care of you. If you let me, I'd do my damnedest to keep you safe and warm and happy for the rest of your life."

His words, and the intense emotion behind them, stunned her. And frightened her. Needing time to gain control, she moved to set her plate down on an upended stump near her chair. She forgot about the duffel on her lap, though, and the whole thing fell to the ground, its contents spilling out into the dirt.

She swore, and Chase knelt beside her to help pick things up. Intent on getting everything back into the bag, she didn't notice him stop and hold the pocketknife she'd found at the poaching site.

"I used to have a knife like this," he said. She looked up and discovered that the knife had somehow fallen out of the evidence bag. She reached for it in a panic, visualizing the damage he could do to the fingerprints that might be on it.

He was too quick, though, and he pulled it away, turning the knife over to read the inscription. Instantly, his face broke into a wide grin. "Hey, this *is* my knife. Jake gave it to me a couple of years ago, right after a freak August blizzard stranded me on the top of Mount Whitney. See, right here. 'Next time you'll be prepared'. The *J* is for *Jake*."

Carly could feel the blood pumping sluggishly through her veins as his words echoed through her mind.

My knife. My knife. My knife.

She couldn't breathe, and she frantically thought back to where she'd found the knife. Right next to the shell casings that had fallen out of the weapons that had butchered a mother bear and her young cub.

The sheer vastness of the Wind Rivers pushed coincidence completely out of the realm of possibility. Whoever had left that knife there had been involved in the killing, and probably in the other bear poaching deaths in the region.

"Where'd you find this?" Chase asked her.

"I . . . I . . ." She couldn't think, couldn't move.

"It must have been in one of the saddlebags, right?" He didn't wait for an answer before continuing. "I lost it early in the spring, and I thought I turned those bags inside out looking for the damn thing, but I guess I missed it somehow."

He grinned again and rose to his feet, pocketing the knife. "Jake will be glad to see this. I'm a thirty-one-year-old man who's well into his second career and he can still make me feel like a little kid in trouble for leaving his grandpa's wrenches outside in the rain. Thanks for finding it, sweetheart."

He leaned across the space between them, and she realized he was going to kiss her. She quickly turned her head just before their lips met, and his kiss landed on her cheek.

He didn't seem to notice, and turned away to start breaking camp.

Carly sat down shakily on the camp chair, her fingers numb. The first shock of horror was beginning to shimmer and fade, dissolving into doubt.

She couldn't believe he was the outlaw she hunted. She *wouldn't* believe it. Not Chase. He might be many things, not the least of them a contrary son of a gun, but he was absolutely, positively, emphatically no poacher. A few days ago, she would have been the first one to suspect him, would have been only too happy to believe him capable of all manner of illegal and immoral activities. But that was before she'd come to know the man he'd become, before she'd glimpsed his compassion, before she'd shared gentle, healing laughter with him, before she'd spent the night wrapped in his heat.

Her gut instinct told her he was innocent, but beyond that, he had no motive. He didn't need the money that usually prompted this kind of poaching. And he had too much love and respect for these mountains and the wildlife that lived there to desecrate them so heinously.

Her breathing slowed and relief spread through her. She replaced the rest of her belongings while she tried to figure out what must have happened.

If he wasn't the poacher, how had his knife ended up at the crime scene?

Perhaps someone—a client, an employee, an enemy—had stolen it and planted it at the site to blame him. Or perhaps that someone had just stolen it and accidentally dropped it there. The problem was, the only fingerprints she was likely to find on the knife now—assuming she could get it back long enough to test for prints—would be his.

The evidence looked damning. Sure, nobody around here would believe Chase could be behind the poachings. But grizzlies were threatened species in the lower forty-eight states, so she was required to work with the U.S. Fish and Wildlife Service on her investigation and had to report all preliminary findings to them.

She would have to find a way to completely clear Chase before those federal investigators stepped in. And she'd have to make darn certain it didn't look like she was covering for him.

The best thing to do, she told herself, would be to pull away from him, to rebuild the barriers between them so she could conduct the investigation without the overwhelming distraction of her feelings for him. She would have to be distant and impartial if she wanted to avoid any appearance of a conflict of interest.

She watched him, looking rough and beautiful and irresistible as he stopped to wrestle with Jackson, and her heart cried out in pain.

How could she do it? How could she return to being polite strangers when all she could remember was the joy of being in his arms?

NINE

Chase couldn't quite figure out what had happened.

One minute Carly had been laughing and joking with him, sweet and affectionate. The next, she'd frozen up colder than spring runoff in a mountain stream.

They'd been riding hard since breakfast, the dry trail helping them make good time, and Chase expected to reach the trailhead and his pickup by dusk. He couldn't say it had been an enjoyable ride, though. Every time he tried to talk to Carly, she responded in colorless monosyllables. A few hours ago he'd been riding abreast of her and had touched her arm to show her something. She'd shrugged him off as if he'd poked her with a hot coal, then spurred Sunny on ahead.

His first reaction had been bewilderment, and he'd spent the next couple of hours examining their whole trip to try to figure out what he'd done to bring her back to this. Now, he was just plain angry at her stubborn refusal to talk to him.

"We'll stop here for lunch," he announced when

they reached a rocky meadow filled with young grass for the horses.

"No," she answered. "I'm not hungry. Let's just keep moving."

It was her longest conversation all morning, and he clenched his hands on the reins in frustration.

"The horses need a rest, so we're stopping," he responded, unable to keep the irritation out of his voice. "If you don't like it, you can just take your skinny little butt off that horse and start walking."

She shrugged, and slid off Sunny's wide back.

With jerky movements, he pulled two sodas and the sandwiches he'd made that morning out of the cooler on the packhorse's back, and tossed one of each to her. She caught them, whistled for Jackson, who'd loped on ahead of them, and walked toward the pines bordering the meadow.

"I need to stretch my legs a bit," she said, without once looking him in the eye. "Go ahead and eat and I'll be back by the time you're ready to move on."

"I'll come with you . . ." he started to say, but she had disappeared into the thick brush. The dog gave Chase a long apologetic look, then bounded after her.

Speechless, Chase stared after them for a few minutes, then in a burst of temper, threw his own sandwich into the dirt and uttered a long string of curses that would have earned him a taste of soap when he was a boy.

"Of all the pigheaded, stubborn women . . ." he growled to the horses, who paid him not the slightest bit of attention as they grazed.

He was getting damn sick and tired of being blamed

for everything that went wrong in her life. He had no doubts that whatever was stuck in her craw somehow harkened back to Mike and that miserable spring.

He ought to just march right after her and lay the truth on the line, he thought. Just tell her, plain as can be, to grow up and deal with the harsh fact that sometimes bad things happen and you can't spend your whole life looking for somebody to be responsible! He ought to tell her every dirty detail about that time, about Mike and Jessie and the stupid, selfish choices his best friend had made that forever altered the course of all their lives.

He ought to, he knew, but he wouldn't, at least not right now. For one thing, he'd promised Jessie. For another, he couldn't bear to cause Carly any more pain, not yet, not when their relationship was built on such shaky ground.

Horseflies descended on his sandwich. Great. Now he was mad *and* hungry. Even as he thought it, he realized his anger had dissipated. All that was left was the thick bile of fear in his mouth.

Carly returned as he was redistributing the weight on the packhorse after he'd choked down a quickly constructed lunch. He heard the dog's bark first, then turned to watch her move slowly toward him.

"How was your walk?" he asked.

She shrugged, still not looking at him. "Nice. We followed the creek for a ways to a big beaver dam. Jackson spooked them, and they smacked the water so loud it turned my big brave dog into a cowering mass of terror."

So she was back to talking to him. Chase didn't know whether to just be grateful for that small kernel of conversation or to kiss her senseless until she dropped the cool, impersonal tone of voice.

Like two strangers, they mounted and headed out, keeping up a polite conversation all afternoon as the horses carried them further and further from the wild passion they'd shared so briefly. They talked about the weather, about people in town they both knew, about Whiskey Creek's annual Founders' Day celebration a few weeks away.

They talked about everything but the emotions that bubbled just below the surface like carbon dioxide waiting for the geyser to blow.

She even asked him about his stupid pocketknife, when he'd seen it last and what he'd been doing. She seemed unusually concerned about it, but hell, he thought, talking about it was better than lapsing into another cold, empty silence.

"It was probably February or March, I guess. I lent it to one of my ranch hands."

"Why would you do that?"

He frowned, trying to remember. "We were out dropping feed during the last big blizzard and he forgot to bring something to cut baling twine from the hay, I think."

"Which ranch hand?"

"Billy Markeson. You know, Sarah and Will's oldest."

"Boy, he must be, what? Nineteen or twenty by now?"

"Nineteen, I think."

"Is he a good kid?"

Chase shrugged. "His mama thinks so."

"But you don't?"

"He's like a lot of kids, I guess. Drinks too much, plays too hard. Thinks the world owes him something."

She studied him curiously. "He seems like an odd sort of ranch hand for you."

"He was. He no longer works at the Lazy Jake."

Her brown eyes suddenly sharpened. "Why not?"

He was silent for a minute. "We had a mutual parting of the ways." He decided not to tell her about the real reasons, the missing tools, the frequent absences, the boy's mocking attitude toward the kids at the Lazy Jake. He'd finally realized he'd have to fire him, when he caught Markeson kicking a horse in the ribs with his sharp-toed cowboy boots after he'd been bucked off.

What the hell did his insignificant personnel problems matter, anyway? he wondered. He should be interrogating Carly about why she'd pushed him away again, why she'd reverted to treating him like a stranger. But fear stilled his questions.

Could he handle her answers?

They reached his pickup and horse trailer just as the sun was setting in vivid flames of red and orange.

High in the mountains they'd left, a coyote called out, looking for companionship: a long, eerie cry that resonated through the hills.

Chills skittered down Chase's spine at the lonely sound. Without Carly in his life, he'd be just like that coyote, he thought, a creature of survival, wandering aimlessly in search of some elusive happiness.

It sounded melodramatic, but the truth of it resonated in his chest. How would he survive if she packed up those chocolate eyes and her smart mouth and headed back to Cheyenne?

He unpacked the horses and loaded them into the trailer. When they were once again riding along in the tight confines of the cab, he realized the time had come to cross whatever ravine she'd dug between them. He lifted his attention from the road for a moment and saw her closing her eyes, her head resting against the seat. The peaceful expression on her face sent a fresh surge of anger coursing through him.

"Don't you dare go to sleep."

Her eyes flew open at his harsh tone, and the stricken pain he saw there doused his anger quicker than anything else could have. What had he done to hurt her?

"Carly, sweetheart, you can't shut me out like this."

"Like what?"

He laughed, a bitter, hollow sound. "Like what? Well, let's see. This morning you awoke in my arms with a smile on your face, and now you flinch like I'm going to hit you if I so much as look at you. Sometime in the hours since the sun came up today, you've gone back to hating my guts and you ought to at least have the nerve to fill me in on whatever the hell I did."

"I don't hate you," she said in a small voice.

"Yeah, well, you're not exactly overflowing with affection here, darlin'."

"I'm sorry," she whispered. "It's just . . . There are a few things I have to work out right now. I promise, nothing's changed. I just need a little time."

He nearly laughed again. Damn right, nothing had changed. They were right back where they had started four days ago.

"Son of a bitch."

Chase slammed the receiver down, then picked the entire phone up and chucked it with all his strength across the Lazy Jake's office.

It hit the rough log wall and fell to the floor, shattering into bits of plastic with wires strewn on the floor like the entrails of some high-tech robot. Throwing it had done nothing to alleviate the fury whipping through him. He was contemplating what else he could throw when Jake poked his head around the corner.

"What in tarnation's gotten into you, boy?" his grandfather asked, bushy eyebrows nearly meeting as he frowned. "That phone you just took your temper out on cost me twenty-nine ninety-nine down at the Wal-Mart in Jackson last year."

"Sorry, Pop." He managed to speak despite the blazing anger roaring inside him. "I'll buy you another one next time I go to town."

Jake pulled up a crumpled piece of metal and glared at his grandson. "Darn right you will. You might have that kind of dough to throw around, so to speak, but this old man's on a fixed income. I'm saving up for my retirement."

If he hadn't been so upset, Chase would have chuckled at his grandfather's righteous indignation. As it was, he barely controlled himself from picking up the computer they used for ranch accounts and throwing it on the floor along with the telephone.

"You want to tell me what kind of bug you got in your britches, boy?"

"No," Chase answered tersely.

"Too bad." Jake perched on the edge of the desk. "I figure I got a right to know what's goin' on, seein' as it's my phone you just did a number on. So to speak," he repeated, chuckling at his bad joke.

"That was Verl Handley, down at Game and Fish, calling to inform us that, as of this morning, Lazy Jake Outfitters is the number one suspect in all the bear poachings that have been going on around here in the last six months."

Jake stared at him for a few seconds, then his shoulders started shaking as laughter rumbled from him.

"Us? Poachers?" Jake laughed again, holding his sides as he leaned toward the floor.

"It's not funny, Pop." Chase ran a hand through his hair. "Being the good friend he is, Verl thought he'd best warn us that he, Carly, and four federal wildlife agents are on their way out here with a search warrant to comb the place for evidence."

Jake slowly straightened, the merriment fading from his expression. "Carly? You mean to tell me our little Carly Jane's gonna let them come out here like we're some kind of criminals?"

"No, I'm not." Acid hurt sharpened his voice. "Our little Carly Jane's not *letting* them do anything. She's riding at the front of the posse, the one holding the noose."

Jake looked puzzled. "Why, that's just plain crazy. Carly oughta know we'd never do anything illegal."

"She ought to," Chase agreed. "Apparently she found some kind of evidence on our little pleasure trip to the Wind Rivers that pins the blame on us."

Later, Chase thought, much, much later, if his anger ever cooled, maybe he'd be able to deal with the pain slicing him into pieces that she could actually believe him capable of this.

Restless and edgy, he rose and strode to the window, shoving his hands in his pockets so he wouldn't be tempted to pound the wall into pieces. At least this apparently solved the mystery of her withdrawal on the trail. In her eyes, he was a poacher, someone who would gun down rare and magnificent animals for a few dollars.

She *loved* him, dammit. He knew it, as sure as he knew those mountains out the window. How could she be pushing this?

"What do you plan to do, son?"

Jake's quiet voice diverted him from the hurt that was beginning to outpunch the anger.

He shrugged, still staring blindly out the window. "Nothing I can do, at least not until I know what she supposedly has on us."

He looked back at his grandfather, wishing the old man could ease this pain as he'd done so many times when Chase was a scared, lonely little boy. Pop was silent, though.

"We'll let them come out and serve their little warrant," Chase said curtly. "Lord knows they won't find anything here. And then I plan to have a nice, long chat with Officer Carly J. Jacobs."

The sound of her pulse beating as loudly and as rapidly as the hoofbeats of a galloping horse echoed in

Carly's ears as she drove the last few miles of the Lazy Jake's rutted private road.

She would have given everything she possessed to avoid this confrontation with Chase. Just imagining his reaction to this search made her lungs refuse to function and nausea bounce through her.

This whole mess was her fault. She should have kept her mouth shut, should have kept her counsel until she found Billy Markeson and interrogated him, until she'd cleared Chase. Instead, she'd stupidly enlisted several other wardens in the Whiskey Creek district to help her find the suddenly elusive suspect, and word had filtered to the federal agents.

She was close, so close, to Markeson. All the evidence pointed to him. In the last four days she'd worked harder than she ever had in her life. She'd discovered Markeson knew the Wind River Range probably as well as Chase. Last fall he'd purchased a weapon of the same caliber and make as the one used in the poachings, and he'd recently made several large deposits in a Jackson bank. The dates of those deposits coincided almost perfectly with each bear death.

Markeson had also flown from Jackson to San Francisco shortly after each poaching incident, and had been seen in Chinatown, a prime market for the bear gallbladders that made the poaching so lucrative. The clincher for her was that two days ago, Markeson bought another plane ticket to San Francisco. She had pulled every string she could find, and there were now four undercover agents staked out at the shop where they believed Markeson's contact worked.

With the mountain of evidence against the boy, how could the federal agents still believe Chase was involved?

The problem was, it was his knife, and it could be his word against Markeson's about who had possession of it just before it showed up at the poaching site. Beyond that, Chase had also made several trips to the Bay area. They didn't coincide all that well with the poachings, but a good prosecutor could make a strong point with them.

Carly flexed her sweaty hands on the steering wheel, touched and astonished and a little overwhelmed once again by the reason behind those visits of Chase's, and by what he was doing at the Lazy Jake.

With a jolt, she realized they were nearly at the ranch. Maybe she could still stop this, she thought frantically. She had to try one last time.

"Look, guys," she said to the two agents riding with her. "I'm telling you again, you're making a big mistake. The Lazy Jake owners are not involved with this ring. I'd stake my reputation on it."

The chief investigator, a burly Montanan named Randy Watkins, frowned at her. "Then we'll find that out when we search the place, won't we?"

"If you can just wait one more day, the Lazy Jake will be completely cleared. I promise."

"In the meantime, if Samuelson is the mastermind, he'll have time to hide every bit of evidence implicating him. Sorry, Jacobs, but we've got to take him by surprise."

"Markeson is our guy. What else do you need, a signed confession?"

"If Markeson is our guy, then Samuelson has nothing to hide, right?"

She was wasting her breath, she thought as she stopped in front of the ranch house. To the feds, she knew, the objections she and Verl had raised reeked of good-old-boy politics, a stonewalling effort to protect the hometown hero. If she didn't know Chase so well, she would have thought the same thing.

Her hands shaking, she set the truck's parking brake and turned off the ignition. Her choices were decidedly limited: stay in the truck and hide like a scared rabbit or get out to face Chase's wrath.

The decision was taken out of her hands when the driver's door flew open and she turned slowly, warily, knowing he would be standing there.

"Smile real pretty and get out like you're just greeting an old friend." He spoke with bitter irony, in an undertone loud enough for only her to hear, since the two federal agents were climbing out the other side. The smile pasted on his face was at grim odds with the look in his eyes, making Carly think of a coiled rattler ready to lash out at anything that moved.

"Chase, don't—"

One big hand encircled her upper arm in a tight grip, and he lifted her out of the cab and to the ground just as Verl and the other agents arrived in another state vehicle.

By the time the men had climbed out and joined them, Carly's fingers were turning numb from his fierce grip on her arm. She barely noticed it, though, as she tried to fight through the misery and longing that had settled around her in a choking cloud.

So much for the element of surprise, she thought. Chase had obviously known they were coming. Jake too. The older man was standing behind Chase, looking understandably confused and worried.

"Officers," Chase said tersely, "this here is my grandfather, Jake Samuelson. He's the owner of the ranch, while I run the guide service. He can show you around and answer any questions. Officer Jacobs and I have a few matters to discuss."

Without waiting for a response, he walked into the lodge, dragging Carly behind him. She practically had to run to keep up with him as he strode to the ranch kitchen.

"Chase, stop this. Let go of me. I mean it."

"Oh, you mean it, do you." He flung her words at her at the same time he dropped his hold on her. "How am I supposed to know what you mean? You sure as hell sounded like you meant it when you begged me to make love to you in that cave."

She'd known this was going to be ugly. If there had been any way to avoid being there while his ranch was searched, she would have done her best to find it. As the investigating officer, though, she'd had no choice but to be present.

"I'm just doing my job, Chase."

"Since the moment you crossed the county line you've been itching to bring me down. I'd say you picked one hell of a way to do it."

She flushed. "If you can just trust me, this will be over soon."

"Trust you? *Trust you?*" He laughed harshly. His anger was a living thing, prowling the room like a caged beast. "That's a real hoot coming from you. Do you even know what the word means?"

"Chase . . ." She faltered, not knowing what to say. She didn't want him to be angry. She wanted his arms around her, wanted to touch her lips to his forehead, to kiss away the lines of fury slashing across it.

She clutched her shaking hands together, willing away a picture of them floating in the hot springs, bodies and souls entangled. Taking a deep breath, she asked the question that had been uppermost in her mind since she learned the truth about what he was doing with the ranch.

"Chase . . . why didn't you tell me about the Lazy Jake?"

"You mean the nice little poaching operation I've got here? Sorry, sweetheart, I guess it never came up."

"I know about Mike's Kids, about the children with juvenile diabetes you've been helping."

In the course of the investigation she'd learned all about the diabetes camp he ran, funded through donations from his former teammates; about the outdoors skills the children were taught with the hope they'd learn not to hate their bodies and the limitations of their disease.

As Mike had done.

"Oh, they're all part of it," Chase said, anger radiating off him. "It's a perfect cover, don't you think? I take the kids out and we scour the whole damn mountains, blasting away at everything that moves. Then we come back and have a nice picnic."

She bit her lower lip to stop its trembling. "Chase,

stop it. Answer my question. Why didn't you tell me about Mike's Kids?"

"You want to know why? Look outside." He dragged her to the window. From there they could see the federal investigators searching the barns while groups of children huddled together, faces white with anxiety.

"See those friends of yours? Face it, Carly, you don't want to believe anything good about me. For the last ten years you've been judging me again and again when I never even had a damn trial. What's the use of defending myself, when you already have your suspicious little mind made up?"

She turned from the window. "That's not fair, Chase."

"You're absolutely right. It's not fair, and I'm sick to death of it." His jaw worked like he wanted to say more, but he finally pivoted and left her standing alone in the warm, yeasty-smelling kitchen, while the sounds of the search continued all around her.

Carly stood there for a long time, praying that the phone would miraculously ring, that Markeson would be caught and the misery would end for all of them. The echo of Chase's words mocked her long after he'd left. She *had* suspected him that day in the mountains. For a minute, maybe even less, she'd judged and convicted him, just as he said.

But she'd tried, hadn't she? Tried to clear his name, to protect him. Apparently she hadn't tried hard enough.

A deep, age-graveled voice spoke to her from the open doorway, distracting her from her grim thoughts.

"Hey there, little girl. What are you doin' in here all by your lonesome?"

Carly looked up to see Jake walking toward her. The smell of peppermint candy and horses thrust her back to her childhood, to a time when Jake and his wife Alice had been her substitute grandparents.

Carly didn't think, she just acted, throwing her arms around his leathery neck and pressing her lips to his dearly familiar wrinkled cheek. He grabbed her in a huge bear hug that lifted her off the floor.

"Jake." Carly couldn't help laughing, despite the unshed tears that turned her eyes gritty. "Put me down, you crazy old man. I'll break your back."

"You? You always were a scrawny little pipsqueak who didn't weigh more than a day-old calf. Let me get a look at this pretty lil' face."

Setting her feet on the floor again, Jake gripped her chin in gnarled hands and turned her toward the light. "Yep. Just like Chase said. You've gone and grown into a real beauty."

Carly blushed and pulled away. "Still full of malarkey, aren't you?"

"No such thing. Yes, sir, I can sure see why that grandson of mine came down out of those mountains looking like somebody poleaxed him."

As if he'd known they were talking about him, Chase walked in, took one look at them, and marched purposefully in their direction. Carly had a vivid image of a hawk guarding his nest as Chase moved between her and his grandfather, looming protectively over the old man.

"Interrogating Jake won't get you anywhere, Officer," he bit out, his voice dripping contempt though his face remained stony.

"I wasn't interrogating anybody," she retorted. "We were just talking."

"Go ahead and sharpen your vicious claws on me, but you leave him out of this. You hear me?"

"Chase," Jake said sternly. "Behave yourself."

His grandson ignored him, still pinning Carly with a steely glare. "He's done nothing to deserve what you're putting him through."

"And you have?" she couldn't help asking.

"My conscience is clean, Carly Jane. How about yours?"

"Chase!" Jake barked. "Leave the girl alone."

Chase gave a harsh laugh. "I'd say she's made it abundantly clear that's what she wants. Don't worry, Officer. Like you said to me one rainy night not too long ago, you stay out of my way and I'll make damn sure I stay out of yours."

Giving Carly one more look of warning, he turned and left the room.

"Don't you worry none about Chase, honey," Jake said. "He'll cool off."

She looked up at his concerned, sweetly aged face and something crumpled inside her.

"No, he won't. He hates me now. I can't say I blame him."

"When that stubborn grandboy of mine figures out he's actin' like a dog with a sore paw, he'll be sorry he lashed out at you."

Carly murmured doubtfully.

"You'll see. You're good for him, and if that boy has half a brain in that thick head of his, he'll figure it out."

She started to answer, but from inside the lodge she

heard the tinny ring of a cellular phone. Her breathing stopped. Was it the undercover agents in Chinatown with Markeson? She had been certain Markeson would show up that day to sell the gallbladders, but after what she had just done to Chase, she wasn't sure she deserved such good fortune. Finally she could stand the suspense no longer.

"I—I'm sorry, Jake. I've got to find Verl."

"Last I seen him, he was in the office. Lemme show you how to get there."

Carly forced herself not to run through the lodge, matching her steps to the old man's slower pace.

When they reached the office, her gaze went immediately to Chase standing beside the desk. He looked up at their entrance and stared back at her, his eyes hard.

"Sorry for the inconvenience," Randy Watkins was saying to Chase, holding out his right hand. "We appreciate your cooperation in light of this little mix-up."

Chase briefly shook the man's hand. "Always glad to do my part for the good guys," he answered, his voice caustic enough to etch glass.

Watkins barely glanced at the damage they had wrought in the room. Books had been pulled from the shelves and lay in sloppy piles, their pages blowing in the breeze from the open window, and jumbled papers covered nearly every inch of the hardwood floor.

"Yes, well," Watkins said, "bill Game and Fish for whatever damages you may have incurred." He caught sight of Carly. "Show's over, Jacobs. We're packing up and heading back to town."

Carly barely heard him. Her attention was focused on Chase, and she died a little inside at the expression he wore when he looked at her: cold as a January morning spent riding fence.

"What happened?" she managed to ask Watkins.

"Our undercover guys just nabbed Markeson trying to fence a couple of fresh gallbladders. Guess you were right, Jacobs."

Relief washed through her, followed by elation, then puzzlement. Why was Chase still looking so angry, then?

"When our guy collared him," Watkins went on, "he popped like a cheap beach ball and confessed everything. Turns out, he and a few of his buddies have been behind all the poaching. At first he tried to blame Samuelson here, but then he broke down and said nobody else at the Lazy Jake was involved."

"Just like Carly told you boys," Verl said, slapping a beefy hand onto Carly's shoulder. "Let's clean up this place."

Watkins left to round up the other agents, and Carly and Verl attempted to put the office back to rights. As they worked, Chase evaded all of her attempts to talk to him. Finally, Jake said they'd done enough and that he'd walk Verl out. That left just Carly and Chase in the office, and she made one last attempt to explain.

"Chase, I'm sorry . . ." She meant to apologize that he'd had to suffer through with the search, that she hadn't been able to find the real culprit quickly enough to protect him, but he cut her off.

"I don't want to hear it."

"Hear what?"

"That you're sorry. That you trusted me all along. All the pretty words you think I want to hear."

"But—"

"Go home, Carly."

She started to try again, but the fury darkening his eyes halted her words.

"And don't come back, right?" she whispered.

"You said it. Not me."

She stared at him for a long moment, then she tilted her chin high and walked out the door.

TEN

Somehow she made it through the rest of the day, though later Carly had almost no recollection of what she did. She numbly endured the graphic poaching stories of the two federal agents as she drove them back to the Whiskey Creek district office, then spent several hours going through paperwork on the case.

At last, just when she felt as if the life inside her had shriveled, leaving only a dried, empty husk, Verl sent her home, wearing a mixed expression of pity and understanding.

In a state of dazed shock, she retraced the same route she'd traveled just hours earlier. She paused at the crossroads between her cabin and the Lazy Jake, and at last the emotions searing her insides forced their way out into the open.

She didn't realize she was crying until she felt a tear drip from her face onto her hand clenched around the steering wheel. For a moment she just stared at the wet spot, struck by how long it had been since anything had loosened the tight grip she kept on her emotions. Too long. Years of emotions rushed to the surface like an uncapped geyser, and she rested her forehead on her folded arms on the wheel as she wept great wrenching sobs.

She cried for the stark, angry pain she'd glimpsed in Chase's eyes, pain she didn't know how to wipe away.

For the empty years that stretched out ahead of her, years without his teasing grin and electric eyes.

For the past and the present and the future.

While she wept, Mother Nature let loose with a violent summer storm, and Carly drove the last few miles through near-blinding rain that slanted against the windshield and thunder that shook her little truck.

She barely made it to the cabin before the roads turned to a slick, dangerous mess. In just the few minutes it took her to walk from the pickup to the woodpile and back to the cabin, she was drenched through and shivering uncontrollably.

Forty-five minutes later she felt physically better, if not mentally. A fire in the fireplace had dispelled most of the chill and she'd managed to choke down a bowl of soup. Still, periodic shivers racked her body and she couldn't seem to loosen the tight band of misery around her heart.

She should do something constructive, she thought, lying in front of the fire with her head on Jackson's back. But try as she might to summon her strength, it was as if all her energy stores had been drained away, leaving her limp and morose.

When had she become such a moody person? she wondered tiredly as she watched the flames dip and sway. She'd always considered herself even tempered, easygoing. The least likely among her circle of friends to pine over a man.

Then again, none of her friends had ever loved and lost a man like Chase Samuelson.

The high whinny of a horse interrupted her thoughts, and she barely missed having her head clunk onto the floor when Jack leaped to his feet. Growling, the dog pranced to the door, sniffed a few times, then quieted, his tail wagging a welcome for whoever waited on the other side.

Chase.

Carly stood there for a long time, her hand on the weathered wood of the door, sensing him on the other side. Was he there for a confrontation or a reconciliation? Her heart pounded painfully in her chest as she waited for his knock. A log shifted on the fire, sending a shower of sparks up the chimney, while Jack's tail thumped like a metronome against the door. After several minutes, the dog finally gave up and plopped back in front of the fire.

And still Chase didn't knock.

What the hell was he doing here? Chase asked himself. He leaned against the porch railing, fingering the barely worn Stetson he'd donned instead of a ball cap, for the added protection it gave against the elements. It felt about as awkward in his hands as he felt standing on Carly's porch.

He shouldn't have come. He should have stayed exactly where he was an hour ago, warm and dry in his office while he pretended to go over ranch accounts. He'd be there now, instead of dripping wet and chilled to the bone from the ride over here, if it hadn't been for Jake.

His grandpop had come in while Chase tried to make sense of the files that had been hopelessly jumbled in the search.

"It's going to take me months to figure out the order these were supposed to be in," he'd muttered to Jake.

"How long's it gonna take for you to figure out you can't live without that little girl you love so much?"

"Pop, I'm not in the mood for a lecture."

"Too dang bad, boy. You're gettin' one, whether you want it or not. Don't be such a stubborn cuss. Go patch things up with her."

Chase stared at him. "Patch things up? Just like that, forget she ever accused me of being something lower than snake guts and kiss and make up? You really think I'm that stupid?"

"You could do worse things."

"Yeah, like jump in front of a moving train, maybe. On second thought, that would probably be a hell of a lot less painful in the long run."

Jake shook his grizzled head. "Worse things like lettin' your dadburned pride keep you as miserable as a chained-up bull on his way to the slaughterhouse. You know, boy, you could search this whole blasted state—hell, the whole dang country—and not find a woman who would love you better than that one does."

"If today's little display of affection is what I can expect from Carly Jacobs, I think I'm better off chained up." He returned to sorting the papers, doing his best to ignore his grandfather's glare.

"You know she knew you weren't no poacher before them agents got that phone call, don't you?"

Chase looked up, startled. Jake sat there like a smug buddha, his arms across his chest and a smirk on his face.

"She what?"

"You were so mad this morning, you didn't even hear what that Watkins fella and Verl said, that Carly knew it was Billy Markeson all along. Accordin' to Verl, that little girl spent the last four days workin' like crazy tryin' to find evidence to save your sorry hide and prove it was Billy that was poachin'."

With that, his grandfather walked out, but he'd planted just enough doubt in Chase's mind to drive him crazy. He spent another hour staring into space, then finally decided he had to see Carly once more, just to find out if Pop was telling the truth or just being an interfering busybody.

Knowing he wouldn't be able to navigate a vehicle through the muck the storm had made of the roads, he'd saddled Rebel and headed through the shortcut to the Jacobs' cabin. What would be a thirty-minute ride by road took him half that using the shortcut.

As he rode through the dismal weather, he couldn't help wondering if this was all an exercise in futility. Even if Carly had come to believe he wasn't a poacher, it was too little, too late. A woman who loved him should never have suspected him in the first place. Still, like the moon inexorably directs the tides, she drew him to her and he was powerless to fight it.

Now he stood on her porch, certain he could hear her breathing on the other side of the door, a riot of feelings whirling through him as he tried to decide whether to knock and face her or melt back into the night.

What the hell, he was already here.

He might as well knock.

She answered the door wearing a ratty old bathrobe he recognized as one he'd seen her father in years ago. With her hair loose and tangled around her face, she looked more like the girl he remembered than the woman he'd come to love.

It was her red and swollen eyes, though, that cracked through his chest to his heart. When had he ever seen her cry? he wondered, then answered his own question. Never. The sight of those cocoa eyes blurring with tears was more than he could stand.

"Aw, Carly. Sweetheart, don't cry." He reached for her and she fell against him, her arms tight around his waist, her face buried in his shirt. She felt slight and fragile in his arms, as if she'd break into little pieces if he moved the wrong way.

They stood that way for a long time while the fire popped and hissed and Jackson snuffled softly in his sleep.

"Chase, I'm so sorry. I tried so hard not to hurt you. I just . . ."

"Shhh. I know. I know." He put his finger against her lips, then felt the blood pool in his groin when she pursed her lips and kissed his finger. He cupped her face in his hands, struggling to tamp down the desire that always bubbled to the surface when she was around. With shaking fingers, he pushed a loose strand of hair back behind her ear, then froze when her lips, cool and moist, pressed against his palm. Without conscious thought, he moved his hand, replacing it with his mouth against hers.

It started as a gentle kiss, meant only for comfort. At the first taste of her, though, he couldn't suppress the thunderous need to touch her, to drink in her sweetness. Her moan of response drove any thought of restraint out of his head.

It had been too long since he held her in the mountains, days that seemed like years since the stormy magic sparked so briefly between them.

Her hands pulled off his slicker and dug into his shirt, tugging the fabric free of his jeans so she could tuck warm fingers against his hips. For several minutes they rediscovered each other, each caress becoming more urgent. He was just about to slide the bathrobe off her shoulders when a little voice in his head stalled his fingers.

Use your brain. This is not the way to get any questions answered.

He shrugged it off. He loved her and she'd apologized, so why did it matter?

What about the next time?

Damn it to everlasting hell. His hands fell to his sides, and he walked over to the fireplace. He couldn't do this, despite the need that curled through him. He loved her too damn much to risk putting himself through this again.

"Why did you stop?" she asked, her voice a husky plea in the night.

Turning, he found her looking soft and warm and tousled from his kisses even while her shy smile tore at his insides like a jagged broken bottle.

She reached for him but stopped when he spoke abruptly. "Carly, I have to go."

"Go where?" she asked, drawing her hands back.

"Home. Town. Anywhere, just away. I shouldn't have come."

He watched as she quickly rebuilt her protective barriers. "I see. I guess that's that. Well, it's been fun, I'm sure. One more for the road, and all that." Her tone was flippant, but her eyes looked dark and stricken.

He clenched his hands to keep from reaching for her. If he touched her again, he knew he'd be lost.

"We're killing each other, Carly. I meant it up in the mountains when I said I loved you. Hell, I've always loved you. My little Carly, with the big eyes and the truckload of grit. You're all I ever wanted. All these years, I think I had it in the back of my mind that someday you'd come back to Whiskey Creek and me, that you'd be able to see beyond your view of the past to the truth. Today just convinced me I was fooling myself."

"About?" The word was clipped, angry, but her hands were trembling as she slid them into the pockets of the old robe.

"I could try for a million years and never be what you want," he said sadly. "I'm a man, Carly. A flesh-and-blood man, not some bigger-than-life hero who never does anything wrong. I'm packed full of human frailties. I'm bullheaded. Sometimes I say stupid things before I really think them through. I don't like to listen to advice, because I usually think I know what's best for everybody else in the world."

"No kidding?" A ghost of a smile tilted one corner of her mouth, then died when he remained grim.

"No kidding. What I'm saying here, Carly, is that I'm about as far from perfect as a man can get."

"I know that. I love you, Chase. Isn't that what's important?"

He closed his eyes, stunned by the impact of her words. He'd known it, but she'd never said it to him before. When he opened his eyes, he watched a crystalline tear slip down her cheek.

He took a ragged breath. "Can you honestly tell me you never once suspected me in the poachings? When you realized that damn knife was mine, did you think I was the bear killer?"

She said nothing, but he could read the truth in her stricken eyes.

"That's what I figured. Carly, what kind of a relationship do you think we could have when every time I screw up, you're ready to believe the worst? I can't live that way, and I don't think you can either."

"Chase, I've forgiven you for what happened to Mike. I did a long time ago."

"Exactly." He spoke more harshly than he'd intended. "That's exactly what I'm talking about. You have magnanimously decided you can pardon me for something that happened a decade ago. What if I told you that, as far as I'm concerned, I did nothing I'm ashamed of, nothing that requires any offer of forgiveness."

Carly stared at him. Did he really have the nerve to be saying this? she wondered.

"You left town with the woman your best friend planned to marry." Against her will, her voice rose. "How can you say you did nothing wrong? Mike loved Jessie, he would have done anything for her, would have carved the moon into little pieces for her if she'd asked him. But you flashed your big league bonus and that damn sexy grin and, sure enough, she followed you like a mare sniffing after the biggest stallion. And you *let* her, knowing you were leaving Mike here with nothing."

He closed his eyes for a brief moment, and she could tell she'd wounded him. When he spoke, his voice was quiet, bleak. "You see what you want to see, Carly. You always have. This is not about what happened back then. This is about you and me and about being able to accept some things on faith, even if you don't understand them."

"Make me understand, Chase. You keep saying that, that there are things I don't know about that spring. Tell me what I don't know. I'm a grown woman now, not some naive little girl who has to be shielded from the truth. Tell me your truth, Chase, because *my* truth is that you turned your back on us."

"Us?"

She was crying again, one tear following another, and she was powerless to stop them. "Me and Mike. We loved you and you betrayed us. You ask me to trust you. Well, I did once. I trusted you with everything I had. I loved you, Chase. I still love you . . . I never stopped, even through the years I hated you. Just tell me what happened!"

"I can't."

"Can't or won't?"

"Both. You know, the hell of it is, Carly, I don't think I should have to tell you. If you loved me like you say you do, you wouldn't require me to break a promise just so you can decide whether I'm worthy of you. Who knows, maybe even if you heard the whole truth, you'd still blame me for Mikey's death. We'd still be in this same damn predicament. You'll never be able to love me, really love me, until you let go and move on."

"So that's your ultimatum. Mike or you, I have to choose. Somehow I knew it would come down to this."

"Hell no! I would never ask you to do such a thing."

"What do you want from me, then?"

"The one thing you're not willing to give, apparently." He shrugged into his oiled slicker and donned the Stetson he'd hung on the hook by the door. "Just like you said. Trust. If you can't trust me about this, you'll never trust me about anything."

She hated the tears she couldn't stop, hated this weakness she was showing him. Hated most that she knew he was right—that even though she'd forgiven him for what he did all those years ago, she didn't know if she'd ever be able to forget it, or if she'd always be waiting for the next blow he would undoubtedly deliver.

"Good-bye, Carly," he said. "I hope you find what you need."

"Did you remember to put the napkins in, dear?"

"Yes, Mother. And the plates and the cups and the silverware and everything else you asked me to put in the basket." Carly smiled at Betsy's habitual worrying. It didn't bother her as much as it used to, she thought, surprised. Maybe she was finally growing up.

Betsy smiled back and patted her hand. Carly covered her mother's smooth hand with her other one and gave a gentle squeeze. They'd been getting along surprisingly well. She even felt a few pangs of regret at leaving her mother alone in Whiskey Creek when she went back to Cheyenne. She was actually going to miss Betsy's fluttering! The events of the last few weeks had mellowed her typical impatience, had shown her how important it was to cling to her loved ones while she could.

As if she'd read Carly's thoughts, Betsy gathered her close for a quick hug, and Carly cherished the familiar comfort of vanilla- and rose-scented skin and her mother's arms.

"I do so wish you didn't have to drive back tomorrow," Betsy said. "It's been such a joy having you here this week."

"It has been," Carly agreed, glad she'd decided to close the cabin a week ago and move home while she wrapped up the loose ends of the case.

Now that it was over, though, there was nothing stopping her from resuming her old job, her old friends, her old life, as if this summer had been just a brief rest on a long and tiring journey.

She could stay, if she wanted to. Verl had offered her a position as chief investigator for the Wind River district office. The idea was not without considerable appeal—living closer to her mother, working in the mountains she loved. Most tempting was the stability, the idea of working out of one place, of immersing herself in the slow, peaceful life of this town where she would be a stranger to no one.

Of course, even as she entertained the idea, she'd known it was absolutely impossible. She didn't possess the strength to survive the trauma of seeing Chase every day—or even occasionally. She wouldn't be able to conceal from him the sharp pain of knowing what they could have shared and never would.

"I promised myself I wouldn't nag you about it," Betsy said, distracting Carly from her sad thoughts. Her mother pulled away and straightened her clothes. "You've made your decision, and I'm sure you feel it's the best one for you. But don't forget, no matter what happens, you always have a home here."

Betsy's eyes looked suspiciously watery, and Carly was surprised by the answering emotion gathering in her chest. "I won't forget. I promise."

Betsy cleared her throat and stood up. "Enough of this maudlin behavior. That parade's going to start without us if we don't get a move on."

"We wouldn't want that, would we?" Carly asked wryly.

She drove her truck so they could pack the bed with their lawn chairs, blankets, picnic basket, and the dozen pies Betsy had been working on all week for the Literary Guild's baked-goods auction.

"Do you remember how your father loved Founders' Day?" Betsy asked as they drove the short distance to town. "He'd spend the whole day at the park, from sunup to after the fireworks show, helping the parade run smoothly, pitching horseshoes in the afternoon, playing baseball with all you children. He crammed more enjoyment into this day than most people fit into a month."

Carly smiled at the memories. Her dad loved people. He had treated everybody in the county—from the lowliest cowpoke to the wildest kids in school to the area's richest ranching families—with the same respect and dignity. It was what had made him a good principal and an even greater example as a father. She saw many of those traits, that same sincerity, in Chase.

Startled at the thought—at any possibility of a similarity between Chase and her father—Carly jerked her foot on the gas. The little truck shot forward, nearly colliding with a group of pedestrians crossing the road.

"Carly!" her mother squeaked.

"Sorry, Mom," she answered automatically, still stunned by her wayward thoughts. Chase and her father? Did they really share any characteristics?

Yes, she answered her own question. Plenty. That same quirky sense of humor. That same ingrained compassion. That same ability to grab enjoyment out of whatever life threw at them.

Her mind still whirring, Carly parked the truck between the short Main Street that the parade—with its twenty floats and one high-school band—would travel, and the city square where most of the events would take place. As she and her mother carried their lawn chairs to their usual spot on the parade route—on the shady side of the county courthouse—everywhere she looked were familiar faces.

Where was Chase? she wondered as she unfolded her chair, a mixture of apprehension and trepidation fluttering in her stomach. He would definitely be there somewhere. Nobody in town missed the Founders' Day celebration unless they wanted to find themselves nominated to the organizing committee for the next year's activities.

The parade was nearly over when she finally saw

him. Over the rickety loudspeaker rigged to the second floor of the town's only bank, the announcer's voice sounded tinny and garbled, as it had for the last forty minutes. She barely heard the words "kids" "camp" and "Samuelson" before the crowd was clapping and cheering harder than they had for the usual crowd-pleasing sheriff's mounted posse.

And there he was.

Riding Rebel, he was surrounded on all sides by the children currently attending camp at the Lazy Jake. She couldn't tear her gaze away from him as fierce longing and bitter regret warred within her.

Clenching her hands together in her lap, she watched him ride past with a little blond-headed girl perched in front of him, holding on tight to the saddlehorn with one hand while she waved wildly with the other.

Chase grinned down at the girl and whispered something in her ear. Whatever it was must have been good, because the child dropped her hold on the saddle and turned to throw her arms around his neck, planting a big, wet kiss on his cheek.

His face reddened as the crowd cheered louder, and Carly felt her heart flip in her chest. A wave of love for him washed through her so powerfully, she had to close her eyes. Still, the image of him and the little girl burned through her eyelids.

While the parade marched on, Carly was lost in the past, reliving a long-forgotten moment in time.

She'd ridden with him like that once, had been held in his arms as they'd taken one of the Lazy Jake's cutting horses to the old Stand-by to fish.

She'd been nine, Chase thirteen, and both of them had been scared to death. Mike had been going through a particularly rough time. He'd been scheduled to undergo tests for kidney failure that day and no one had been sure what the future held.

She replayed the scene in her mind, stunned that she remembered it so vividly and that she'd ever forgotten it in the first place. Since one of Chase's sisters had been her best friend, Carly had stayed with his family while her parents were down in Jackson with Mike. She'd been in the kitchen of the Lazy Jake waiting for Chase to come home from baseball practice. He'd taken one look at her white, scared face and turned back around to go saddle a horse. They'd been riding for several minutes before she finally had the nerve to ask him the question that had haunted her all day.

"Chase? What if . . . what if Mikey dies?"

His response had been fierce and impassioned. "He's not gonna die. We won't let him."

"But Mom and Dad said he's real sick. He may need a new kidney bean or somethin' like that."

Chase gave her a tight hug and spurred the horse harder. "Don't sweat it, pumpkin," he said. "I've got two 'kidney beans.' I asked my biology teacher about it today, and he said you only need one of them to live on. If Mikey needs another one, we can just give him one of mine. He'd get more use out of it than I would, and I won't even miss it."

With the faith of a child, she hadn't even questioned his logic, had just turned in his arms exactly like that girl had today and hugged him as tight as she could. That was the kind of friendship the two boys had shared, deep and pure and true.

"Carly? Honey, is something wrong?" Her mother's voice severed the connection to the past, and Carly blinked a few times to clear her thoughts.

"I . . . No . . . I just . . ."

Betsy's curious expression melted into one of concern. "I knew this would happen. The minute you walked out of the house without a hat, I knew you were going to have heat stroke before the day was through. It's your coloring, honey. Blondes can't be too careful."

She reached over to place a hand on Carly's forehead. "Hmmm. You don't feel feverish, but why don't we get you over to that bit of shaded grass over there and let you lie down for a moment, just to be on the safe side."

Carly managed a weak chuckle. "I don't have heat stroke, Mother. It's barely eleven o'clock in the morning, and a cloudy day besides. But thanks for worrying about me."

"I'm your mother. It's my job to worry about you. And I have been, especially the last few weeks." Betsy touched her arm. "I've never seen you so unhappy. I just wish I could help."

Carly stared, unseeing, as a procession of shiny new hayracks and threshers drove past, the entry from the local farm implement store. She couldn't shake the image of a younger Chase swearing to do anything he could to save the life of his best friend.

Could a few short years and a conniving woman turn that friendship into ashes? With a shock that seared clear through to her toes, she realized that for the first time in ten years, she was actually questioning the events of that spring.

"Mom," she asked urgently, "why didn't you ever blame Chase for Mikey's death?"

Betsy sighed. "Are we back to that again? Let it go, Carly. It was a long time ago, and no good can come of rehashing it over and over."

"Just tell me." She was nearly frantic with the need to know. "Not once, in all these years, have you said anything negative about Chase. But you had to have seen how devastated Mike was when Chase and Jessie took off. Why don't you blame him?"

Weariness clouded her mother's eyes. "Because I knew how much Chase and Jessie both loved Mike. I never believed either of them had it in them to cheat on Mike together. Whatever their reasons for going away together, I have never been able to believe they did it to betray your brother. Chase is a good man, Carly. A good, honest, sincere man."

A good, honest, sincere man.

He was, she realized. All this time, her brain had been trying to figure out what her heart had already known. She'd been agonizing about how she could possibly love a man who would do such a thing, when what she should have been asking herself was, how could she still believe it after she'd come to know the kind of man he was?

A sweet peace settled over her. It had never been Chase she'd been fighting, Chase she hadn't trusted. Just herself and her own instincts.

"Mother? I have to find Chase. Where would he be?"

Betsy took one look at Carly and smiled. She pulled her daughter into a tight embrace. "Looks like you might be staying around after all, am I right?"

"I don't know. I guess that's up to him," Carly said against her mother's cheek. She pulled away, anxious to resolve this. "Where can I find him?"

"Try the Lion's Club hamburger booth. He usually helps out there after the parade."

She was halfway down the street before her mother finished speaking.

ELEVEN

After fighting her way through the postparade crowds, Carly finally found Chase taking his turn at the grill, wearing a red-striped apron and laughing and flirting with old Mrs. Jensen, who had to be eighty if she was a day.

The elderly woman was blushing and batting her eyes at Chase, and Carly fell in love with him all over again. Her muscles liquified when he took off his cap and wiped away perspiration with his forearm.

When he put it back on, his eyes met hers through the smoke swirling off the grill, and the hand holding the spatula dropped to his side.

Slowly she forced herself toward the big half-barrel barbecue. Grabbing a paper plate, she thrust it toward him.

"I—I'd like a cheeseburger, please," she murmured.

His gaze stayed locked with hers, and she thought she glimpsed something tortured in his eyes before his expression became shuttered again and he looked away.

"How would you like that cooked, ma'am?" he asked.

She smiled at his polite tone and at the way everybody within earshot watched them avidly.

"I'll take it any way you want to fix it," she answered. "I know you're a good cook, so I'll just have to trust you to give me the best you've got."

His gaze flew back to hers, electric-blue depths glittering in the noonday sun. She mustered every bit of courage she had as she faced him, hoping he could see at least a portion of the love she felt for him.

"What if I put something on it that doesn't agree with you?" he asked hoarsely.

Carly couldn't seem to stop smiling as a slow warmth seeped through places that had been too cold for too long. "I'll live through it, especially since I know you're not the kind of man who would deliberately hurt a woman who loves you."

He had the apron off and was reaching for her before she finished the sentence. His fingers gripped her head to angle it for his mouth, and she flung her arms around his neck, laughing and kissing and loving him, feeling as if she'd finally come home.

It was only after he lifted his head that she remembered where they were, remembered their audience that was now clapping and whistling enthusiastically.

Her blush mirrored Mrs. Jensen's—who, she noticed, was beaming along with everyone else in the vicinity—and she slid down until her feet touched earth again.

"Larry," Chase called, "you'll have to finish these

without me." He began to pull Carly away from the crowd.

"Yeah, we can all see you've got bigger burgers to fry," somebody shouted, and Chase laughed, a deep, hearty laugh that vibrated through her, shaking away the last of her uncertainties.

"Damn right," he said.

They were just on the edge of the park, all but ignoring the greetings that came at them from all sides, lost in the simple joy of being together with no conflicts between them, when a youthful voice called after them.

"Uncle Chase, Uncle Chase, wait up."

Chase froze, then turned slowly. Carly turned, too, and watched a dark-haired boy who looked to be about nine running toward them. "Why, Josh Taylor," Chase said. "What are you doing in Whiskey Creek?" The boy flung himself into Chase's arms before Carly got more than a brief glimpse of dark eyes and a sweet smile that seemed oddly familiar. The boy stepped away, an abashed look on his face at being caught hugging someone at his age.

"Carly, this here is Josh Taylor. You know his mama, I think." Chase's eyes sent her an unreadable message. "Jessie Palmer."

She started, staring hard at the boy, then felt the blood leave her face.

No wonder he looked familiar. She'd sat across from that face at the supper table every day for the first seventeen years of her life. A glint of silver caught the sun and her attention, and she saw the medical ID bracelet on his wrist with its red caduceus. She didn't need to see the other side to know what it would say. Diabetes, just like the one the boy's father had worn.

Her brother.

She had no time to assimilate the information, to absorb the shock. A graceful, well-dressed woman came striding toward them, a warm smile on her face.

"Jess!" A wealth of affection was in Chase's voice, and he hugged her tightly. "Why didn't you tell me you were coming back?"

"We wanted to surprise everyone. It's been so long since my folks have seen Josh and Kyle, so we decided to come to Whiskey Creek for Founders' Day."

"I'm glad," he said softly. "It was way past time for you to come home and face whatever kept you away for so long."

"I know," she answered, then caught sight of Carly. Jessie aimed a friendly smile at her, a smile that froze, then melted away when she realized Carly's identity. "You're . . . Hello, Carly," she said.

Carly couldn't pull her stunned gaze from the boy who wore Mike's face to look at the woman she'd once believed would become her sister-in-law.

She didn't see Jess take in her shock, but she vaguely registered the other woman's words to her son. "Why don't you go back and tell Kyle and your dad we found Chase," she ordered quietly. She watched him walk away, before turning back to Carly and Chase.

"You never told her," Jessie said to Chase, disbelief in her voice and in her expression.

"You begged me not to," he reminded her.

"I know, but that was a decade ago. You told me even back then that I wasn't being fair to Mike's family, that I should let them know about our child. I was sure you'd decided Josh has been a secret for too long."

"It wasn't my place to decide that. Whatever my feelings might be, you're his mother."

"Yeah, right, and you're just some schmuck who happened to have an extra bedroom to give to a scared, pregnant nineteen-year-old kid with no place else to go, who bullied me into getting better when I started to miscarry. Just some casual bystander who decided to spend the day holding my hand and coaching me as I bawled through twenty hours of back labor, despite the fact that it almost got you kicked off the team for missing a playoff game."

Carly couldn't take any more. She was going to be sick, she thought. Completely and totally sick all over Jessie Palmer. "I've got to go," she mumbled, and took off through the crowd.

Blind instinct led her to her pickup, and somehow she managed to start it and drive through the lingering throngs. Only after several minutes did her frantic breathing begin to slow.

Without being consciously aware of what she was doing, she found herself at their fishing spot. The wind in the pines whispered its familiar lonesome song as she stumbled down to the river, but she knew only the throbbing of her pulse in her ears and the frenzied tumult of her thoughts.

Mike and Jessie had a son.

And Chase knew. He had always known. Carly staggered to a boulder and leaned against it, her arms clasped protectively around her stomach. Oh, dear Lord. Chase must have taken Jessie to California so she could have the child away from the damning eyes and small-town minds of Whiskey Creek.

He hadn't betrayed them, after all.

With a muffled sob, she slid down the length of the boulder, curling into herself. All this time wasted, the empty years spent in needless hate. She'd been so self-righteous, so damn condemning. And he'd never put forward a word in his own defense. He'd absorbed her accusations and her blame without once telling her the simple words that would have exonerated him.

That was how Chase found her, huddled against the boulder as if the river that flowed along several feet from her threatened to reach out and suck her away.

He stood watching her for a few minutes and knew the instant she realized he was there. She stiffened and gradually unfolded herself to face him.

"Why didn't you tell me?" she asked hoarsely, her eyes blurred with confusion and pain.

He knelt beside her. "I told myself it was because I promised Jess I wouldn't. But I think it was more because I didn't know how. The words never seemed to fit together."

"Why didn't you just try, 'Carly, your brother was a first-class bastard who didn't want his own child'? That must have been what happened, right?"

He said nothing, trying to word things just right, and Carly pounded a fist into the boulder behind her. "I have got to be the most idiotic person on earth. All this time, you've been protecting him, haven't you, just like you always did? Protecting his memory like you tried to protect him when you were boys, always making sure he checked his blood-sugar levels and ate what he was supposed to."

"It wasn't like that," he said softly. "Don't turn against him, please, sweetheart. I have to believe Mike wanted the baby. He loved Jess, but I think he was just so young and terrified about his child inheriting diabetes that he didn't think rationally. You know Mike hated his disease, hated knowing how short his life might be, hated having to be constantly alert, always anxious."

"What—what really happened?"

Chase dreaded hurting her, but he knew she deserved to know the truth finally.

"Jess was thrilled when she found out she was pregnant. They'd planned to marry after he graduated from college, and she figured this would just hurry their plans along a few months. But when she told him—all along expecting him to be as excited as she was—Mike blew up. He said he didn't want to put any child through what he'd lived with."

"Oh, Mikey," Carly whispered. "Was it really so bad for you?"

Aching for her, Chase pulled her into his arms and held her tight, her cheek pressed against his chest.

"Jessie thinks he was in worse shape than he let anybody know about," he said after a few minutes. "She believes he knew his condition was declining and he wanted to push her away, make a sharp break, so she would come to hate him, instead of putting her through the hell of standing by helplessly while he died by inches."

"You were his best friend. What do you think?"

He shrugged. "It fits. Jess called me after he told her

to have an abortion, hoping I could talk some sense into him, but Mike wouldn't even talk about it. He just kept pleading with me to take care of her and saying, 'It's better this way.' Whatever the hell that meant."

"So even though you were beginning a new life in the major leagues, you burdened yourself with a pregnant nineteen-year-old girl."

Chase looked away. "I didn't know what else to do. Jessie couldn't bear to stay in Whiskey Creek, not with Mike here. I've wanted to tell you about Josh so many times. He's so much like Mike, with the same dogged determination and the same ability to take charge of every situation, even though he's only nine years old. I promised her, though, Carly. She didn't want you or your folks to go through the pain of knowing Mike didn't want the baby."

"I treated you so badly," Carly said. "That's what hurts the most, that I wasted so much time being bitter and mean. Why don't you hate me?"

Chase tightened his hold on her and pressed a kiss to the top of her head. "Shhh. How could I hate you? You're my sweet Carly. It was sheer stubborn pride that made me expect you to blindly trust me at the same time that I didn't trust your ability to handle the truth."

"I did trust you, Chase. That's what I was trying to tell you today. It hit me when I watched you in that parade that I always knew, deep down, that Mike's death wasn't your fault. It was just easier blaming you than it was to face the fact that Mike was on a self-destructive course that had nothing to do with any of us."

"I wish I could have spared you that," he said quietly.

"What happens now?"

"Jess said she wants to tell Betsy about Josh herself. I think she wanted to tell her a long time ago, but she didn't want to disrupt Josh's life before he was old enough to understand what had happened."

Carly managed a laugh. "When she gets over the shock, Mother is going to be absolutely delirious about having a grandson to fuss over. Maybe she'll get off my back for at least a couple of months about giving her grandbabies."

Chase chuckled. "We can always give her what she wants. Unless you want to wait a while after we're married before we start a family."

Her heart fluttered, and she stared at him. "After we're what?"

"I'm being arrogant again, aren't I?" he said, smiling. "Sorry. But you know, you have to marry me. I'm not letting you out of my arms again, and Jake and Betsy would no more let us live together than they would both pack up and move away from Whiskey Creek."

Carly didn't blink, afraid that if she did this dream would shimmer away. "Mar-marriage? Are you sure?"

"Unless, of course, you *want* those two busybodies to move away. On second thought, that's not such a bad idea, now that I think about it." He grinned that adorable grin of his. "Let's move in together and see how long it takes them to leave town."

She laughed. "Chase. I'm serious. Marriage is forever."

"That's the idea." He spoke solemnly, all traces of humor gone as his arms tightened around her. "I love you, Carly Jane Jacobs. More than I ever dreamed it was possible to love a woman. I can't guarantee you'll get such a great bargain if you marry me, but I can promise I'll do whatever it takes to keep you happy."

Carly closed her eyes, feeling a sweet contentment settle over her like a warm quilt. Everything in her life came down to this moment, this man. Nothing else seemed important, only his arms, his words, his love.

She smiled into his chest, then opened her eyes and tilted her head to meet his heated gaze. "Pretty words, Samuelson, but you forgot one little detail."

"What would that be?"

"My understanding of the contract we entered into years ago requires me to beat you at arm wrestling in order to win your hand in marriage. I'm not sure I'm woman enough for you."

He laughed huskily. "I'd say you're about ten steps beyond woman enough for me. I thought I'd save all our wrestling for our wedding night, but if you insist . . ." Rolling up his shirtsleeve, he placed an elbow on the boulder.

Had life ever been so completely wonderful? Carly wondered as she knelt on the other side of the rock and gripped his big hand in hers. He squeezed tightly and took a deep breath. "One. Two. Three. Go."

Summoning all her strength, Carly pushed against him. At first she encountered resistance, then in a wild rush his knuckles were hitting the boulder.

"I guess I'm stuck with you," Chase said, grinning. He pulled her across the boulder and back into the haven of his arms.

This was where she wanted to be, she thought. Right here, with him, in this beautiful, wild place where they'd been raised.

"I guess you are," she answered, just before his mouth met hers.

THE EDITORS' CORNER

Fall is just around the corner, but there's one way you can avoid the chill in the air. Cuddle up with the LOVESWEPT novels coming your way next month. These heart-melting tales of romance are guaranteed to keep you warm with the heat of passion.

Longtime LOVESWEPT favorite Peggy Webb returns with a richly emotional tale of forbidden desire in **INDISCREET,** LOVESWEPT #802. Bolton Gray Wolf appears every inch a savage when he arrives to interview Virginia Haven, but the moment she rides up on a white Arabian stallion, challenge glittering in her eyes, he knows he will make her his! Even as his gaze leaves her breathless, Virginia vows he'll never tame her; but once they touch, she has no choice but to surrender. Peggy Webb offers a spectacular glimpse into the astonishing mysteries of love in a tale of fiery magic and unexpected miracles.

Marcia Evanick delivers her award-winning blend of love and laughter in **SECOND-TIME LUCKY**, LOVESWEPT #803. Luke Callahan arrives without warning to claim a place in Dayna's life, but he reminds her too much of the heartbreak she'd endured during her marriage to his brother! Luke wants to help raise her sons, but even more, he wants the woman he's secretly loved for years. Dared by his touch, drawn by his warmth to open her heart, Dayna feels her secret hopes grow strong. In a novel that explores the soul-deep hunger of longing and loneliness, Marcia Evanick weaves a wonderful tapestry of emotion and humor, dark secrets and tender joys.

A love too long denied finds a second chance in **DESTINY STRIKES TWICE**, LOVESWEPT #804, by Maris Soule. Effie Sanders returns to the lake to pack up her grandmother's house and the memory of summers spent tagging along with her sister Bernadette . . . and Parker Morgan. With his blue eyes and lean, tanned muscles, Parker had always been out of Effie's reach, had never noticed her in the shadow of her glamorous sister. Never—until an older, overworked Parker comes to his family's cottage to learn to relax and finds the irrepressible girl he once knew has grown up to become a curvy, alluring woman. And suddenly he is anything but relaxed. Maris Soule has created a story that ignites with fiery desire and ripples with tender emotion.

And finally, Faye Hughes gives the green light to scandal in **LICENSED TO SIN**, LOVESWEPT #805. In a voice so sensual it makes her toes curl, Nick Valdez invites Jane Steele to confess her secrets, making her fear that her cover has been blown! But she knows she's safe when the handsome gambler then suggests they join forces to investigate rigged games at a riverboat casino. She agrees to his scheme, knowing that sharing close quarters with Nick will be risky temptation. In this blend of steamy romance and fast-paced adventure, Faye Hughes reveals the tantalizing pleasures of playing dangerous games and betting it all on the roll of the dice.

Happy reading!

With warmest wishes,

Beth de Guzman   Shauna Summers
Senior Editor   Editor

P.S. Watch for these Bantam women's fiction titles coming in September. With her mesmerizing voice and spellbinding touch of contemporary romantic suspense, Kay Hooper wowed readers and reviewers alike with her Bantam hardcover debut, **AMANDA**—and it's soon coming your way in paperback. Nationally bestselling author Patricia Potter shows her flair for humor and warm emotion in **THE MARSHAL AND THE HEIRESS**; this one has a western lawman lassoing the bad guys all the way in Scotland! From Adrienne deWolfe, the author *Ro-*

mantic Times hailed as "an exciting new talent," comes **TEXAS LOVER,** the enthralling tale of a Texas Ranger, a beautiful Yankee woman, and a houseful of orphans. Be sure to see next month's LOVESWEPTs for a preview of these exceptional novels. And immediately following this page, preview the Bantam women's fiction titles on sale *now*!

Don't miss these extraordinary books
by your favorite Bantam authors

On sale in July:
PRINCE OF
SHADOWS
by Susan Krinard

WALKING RAIN
by Susan Wade

No one could tame him. Except a woman
in love.

From the electrifying talent of
Susan Krinard
author of *Star-Crossed* and *Prince of Wolves*
comes a breathtaking, magical new
romance
PRINCE OF SHADOWS

"Susan Krinard has set the standard for
today's fantasy romance."—*Affaire de Coeur*

*Scarred by a tragic accident, Alexandra Warrington has
come back to the Minnesota woods looking for refuge and a
chance to carry on her passionate study of wolves. But her
peace is shattered when she awakes one morning to find a
total stranger in her bed. Magnificently muscled and perfectly naked, he exudes a wildness that frightens her and a
haunting fear that touches her. Yet Alex doesn't realize
that this handsome savage is a creature out of myth, a wolf
transformed into a man. And when the town condemns
him for a terrible crime, all she knows is that she is dangerously close to loving him and perilously committed to
saving him . . . no matter what the cost.*

The wolf was on his feet again, standing by the door.
She forgot her resolve not to stare. Magnificent was
the only word for him, even as shaky as he was. He

lifted one paw and scraped it against the door, turning to look at her in a way that couldn't be misunderstood.

He wanted out. Alex felt a sudden, inexplicable panic. He wasn't ready. Only moments before she'd been debating what to do with him, and now her decision was being forced.

Once she opened that door he'd be gone, obeying instincts older and more powerful than the ephemeral trust he'd given her on the edge of death. In his weakened state, once back in the woods he'd search out the easiest prey he could find.

Livestock. Man's possessions, lethally guarded by guns and poison.

Alex backed away, toward the hall closet, where she kept her seldom-used dart gun. In Canada she and her fellow researchers had used guns like it to capture wolves for collaring and transfer to new homes in the northern United States. She hadn't expected to need it here.

Now she didn't have any choice. Shadow leaned against the wall patiently as she retrieved the gun and loaded it out of his sight. She tucked it into the loose waistband of her jeans, at the small of her back, and started toward the door.

Shadow wagged his tail. Only once, and slowly, but the simple gesture cut her to the heart. It was as if he saw her as another wolf. As if he recognized what she'd tried to do for him. She edged to the opposite side of the door and opened it.

Biting air swirled into the warmth of the cabin. Shadow stepped out, lifting his muzzle to the sky, breathing in a thousand subtle scents Alex couldn't begin to imagine.

She followed him and sat at the edge of the porch

as he walked stiffly into the clearing. "What are you?" she murmured. "Were you captive once? Were you cut off from your own kind?"

He heard her, pausing in his business and pricking his ears. Golden eyes held answers she couldn't interpret with mere human senses.

"I know what you aren't, Shadow. You aren't meant to be anyone's pet. Or something to be kept in a cage and stared at. I wish to God I could let you go."

The wolf whuffed softly. He looked toward the forest, and Alex stiffened, reaching for the dart gun. But he turned back and came to her again, lifted his paw and set it very deliberately on her knee.

Needing her. Trusting her. Accepting. His huge paw felt warm and familiar, like a friend's touch.

Once she'd loved being touched. By her mother, by her grandparents—by Peter. She'd fought so hard to get over that need, that weakness.

Alex raised her hand and felt it tremble. She let her fingers brush the wolf's thick ruff, stroke down along his massive shoulder. Shadow sighed and closed his eyes to slits of contentment.

Oh, God. In a minute she'd be flinging her arms around his great shaggy neck. *Wrong, wrong.* He was a wolf, not a pet dog. She withdrew her hands and clasped them in her lap.

He nudged her hand. His eyes, amber and intelligent, regarded her without deception. Like no human eyes in the world.

"I won't let them kill you, Shadow," she said hoarsely. "No matter what you are, or what happens. I'll help you. I promise." She closed her eyes. "I've made promises I wasn't able to keep, but not this time. Not this time."

Promises. One to a strange, lost boy weeping over the bodies of two murdered wolves. A boy who, like the first Shadow, she'd never found again.

And another promise to her mother, who had died to save her.

The ghost of one had returned to her at last.

The wolf whined and patted her knee, his claws snagging on her jeans. A gentle snow began to fall, thick wet flakes that kissed Alex's cheeks with the sweetness of a lover. She turned her face up to the sky's caress. Shadow leaned against her heavily, his black pelt dusted with snowflakes.

If only I could go back, she thought. Back to the time when happiness had been such a simple thing, when a wolf could be a friend and fairy tales were real. She sank her fingers deeper into Shadow's fur.

If only—you were human. A man as loyal, as protective, as fundamentally honest as a wolf with its own. A man who could never exist in the real world. A fairy-tale hero, a prince ensorcelled.

She allowed herself a bitter smile. The exact opposite of Peter, in fact.

And you think you'd deserve such a man, if he did exist?

She killed that line of thought before it could take hold, forcing her fingers to unclench from Shadow's fur. "What am I going to do, Shadow?" she said.

The wolf set his forepaws on the porch and heaved his body up, struggling to lift himself to the low platform. Alex watched his efforts with a last grasp at objectivity.

Now. Dart him now, and there will still be time to contact the ADC. She clawed at the dart gun and pulled it from her waistband.

But Shadow looked up at her in that precise moment, and she was lost. "I can't," she whispered. She let her arm go slack. The dart gun fell from her nerveless fingers, landing in the snow. She stared at it blindly.

Teeth that could rend and tear so efficiently closed with utmost gentleness around her empty hand. Shadow tugged until she had no choice but to look at him again.

She knew what he wanted. She hesitated only a moment before opening the door. Shadow padded into the cabin and found the place she had made for him by the stove, stretching out full-length on the old braided rug, chin on paws.

"You've made it easy for me, haven't you?" she asked him, closing the door behind her. "You're trapped, and I can keep you here until . . . until I can figure out what to do with you."

The wolf gazed at her so steadily that she was almost certain that he'd known exactly what he was doing. She wanted to go to him and huddle close, feel the warmth of his great body and the sumptuous texture of his fur. But she had risked too much already. In the morning she'd have to reach a decision about him, and she knew how this would end—how it must end—sooner or later.

Shadow would be gone, and she'd be alone.

Feeling decades older than her twenty-seven years, Alex took her journal from the kitchen and retreated into the darkness of her bedroom. She paused at the door, her hand on the knob, and closed it with firm and deliberate pressure.

She stripped off her clothes and hung them neatly in the tiny closet, retrieving a clean pair of long underwear. The journal lay open on the old wooden bed table, waiting for the night's final entry.

It's ironic, Mother. I thought I'd become strong. Objective. I can't even succeed in this.

Her flannel bedsheets were cold; she drew the blankets up high around her chin, an old childhood habit she'd never shaken. Once it had made her feel safe, as if her mother's own hands had tucked her in. Now it only made her remember how false a comfort it truly was.

It was a long time before she slept. The sun was streaming through the curtains when she woke again. She lay very still, cherishing the ephemeral happiness that came to her at the very edge of waking.

She wasn't alone. There was warmth behind her on the bed, a familiar weight at her back that pulled down the mattress. The pressure of another body, masculine and solid.

Peter. She kept her eyes closed. It wasn't often that Peter slept the night through and was still beside her when she woke. And when he was . . .

His hand brushed her hip, hot through the knit fabric of her long underwear. When Peter was with her in the morning, it was because he wanted to make love. She gasped silently as his palm moved down to the upper edge of her thigh and then back up again, drawing the hem of her top up and up until he found skin.

Alex shuddered. It had been so long. Her belly tightened in anticipation. Peter wanted her. He *wanted* her. His fingers stroked along her ribs with delicate tenderness. They brushed the lower edge of her breast. Her nipples hardened almost painfully.

The arousal was a release, running hot in her blood. In a moment she would roll over and into his arms. In a moment she'd give herself up to the sex, to the searing intensity of physical closeness, seizing it for as long as it lasted.

But for now Peter was caressing her gently, without his usual impatience—taking time to make her ready, to feed her excitement—and she savored it. She wouldn't ruin the moment with words. Peter wasn't usually so silent. He liked talking before and after making love. About his plans, his ambitions. Their future.

All she could hear of him now was his breathing, sonorous and steady. His palm rested at the curve of her waist, the fingers making small circles on her skin.

His fingers. Callused fingers. She could feel their slight roughness. Blunt at the tips, not tapered. Big hands.

Big hands. Too big.

Wrongness washed through her in a wave of adrenaline. She snapped open her eyes and stared at the cracked face of the old-fashioned alarm clock beside the bed. Granddad's alarm clock. And beyond, the wood plank walls of the cabin.

Not the apartment. Her cabin. Not the king-size bed but her slightly sprung double.

The hand at her waist stilled.

Alex jerked her legs and found them trapped under an implacable weight. A guttural, groaning sigh sounded in her ear.

Very slowly she turned her head.

A man lay beside her, sprawled across the bed with one leg pinning the blankets over hers. A perfectly naked, magnificently muscled stranger. His body was curled toward her, head resting on one arm. His other hand was on her skin. Straight, thick black hair shadowed his face.

Alex did no more than tense her body, but that was enough. The man moved; the muscles of his torso and flat belly rippled as he stretched and lifted his head. Yellow eyes met her gaze through the veil of his hair.

Yellow eyes. Clear as sunlight, fathomless as ancient amber. Eyes that almost stopped her heart.

For an instant—one wayward, crazy instant—Alex *knew* him. And then that bizarre sensation passed to be replaced with far more pragmatic instincts. She twisted and bucked to free her legs and shoved him violently, knocking his hand from her body. His eyes widened as he rocked backward on the narrow bed, clawed at the sheets and rolled over the far edge.

Alex tore the covers away and leaped from the bed, remembering belatedly that she'd left the dart gun outside, and Granddad's old rifle was firmly locked away in the hall closet. She spun for the door just as the man scrambled to his feet, tossing the hair from his eyes. Her hand had barely touched the doorknob when he lunged across the bed and grabbed her wrist in an iron grip.

Treacherous terror surged in her. She lashed out, and he caught her other hand. She stared at the man with his strange, piercing eyes and remembered she was not truly alone.

A wolf slept just beyond her door. A wolf that had trusted and accepted her as if she were a member of his pack. One of his own kind. A wolf that seemed to recognize the name she had given him.

"Shadow," she cried. It came out as a whisper. "Shadow!"

The man twitched. The muscles of his strong jaw stood out in sharp relief beneath tanned skin, and his fingers loosened around her wrists for one vital instant.

Alex didn't think. She ripped her arms free of his grasp, clasped her hands into a single fist, and struck him with all her strength.

Haunting, compelling, and richly
atmospheric, this dazzling novel of
romantic suspense marks the impressive
debut of a talented new author.

WALKING RAIN

by Susan Wade

*Eight years with a new name and a new identity had not
succeeded in wiping out the horrors of the past. It was time
for Amelia Rawlins to go home. Home to the New Mexico
ranch where she had spent her childhood summers. Home
to the place where she could feel her grandfather's spirit
and carry on the work he had loved. But someone knew
that Amelia had come back—Amelia, who should have
died on that long-ago day . . . who should have known
better than to think she could come back and start over
with nothing more than a potter's wheel, a handful of
wildflower seeds, and a stubborn streak. And someone was
out to see that Amelia paid in full for her crimes. . . .*

She drove up U.S. 54 from Interstate 10 because that
was the way she had always come to the ranch. Her
old pickup had held up well on the long drive from
the East Coast, but now it rattled and jounced along
the battered road. Amelia checked the rearview mirror often, making certain her potter's wheel was still
securely lashed to the bed of the truck. It was her
habit to watch her back.

She'd reached El Paso late in the afternoon and

stopped there to put gas in the truck. Between that stop and all the Juarez traffic, it was getting on toward evening by the time she left the city and, with it, the interstate. Now the mountains of the Tularosa basin rose on either side of the two-lane road: the soaring ridge of the Guadalupes to her east and the Organ Mountains, drier, more distant, to her west. The eastern range was heavily snowed, peaks gleaming pink in the fading light, and the evening sky was winter-brilliant. Narrow bands of clouds glowed like flamingo feathers above the Organs.

She had forgotten the crystalline stillness of the air here, forgotten the sunny chill of a New Mexico winter. How had that happened? Maybe that was the price she'd paid for forgetting the things she had to forget. Part of the price.

The sun flamed on the horizon, looking as if it would flow down the mountains to melt the world, and then it sank. Its light faded quickly from the sky; already the stars were taking their turn at ruling the deep blue reaches. Amelia rolled down her window, even though the temperature outside was plunging toward freezing. The desert smelled pungent and strong, and there was a hint of pine and piñon on the wind.

It was the wind that whipped tears to her eyes. Certainly the wind; she was not a woman who wept. But she was suddenly swept by a brilliant ache of homesickness—here, now, when she was very near the only home left to her—it caught at her violently. So violently that she almost turned the truck around and went away again.

To need something so much frightened her.

But she was tired, and she had only decided to come here when she could no longer face starting over somewhere new. She'd been rootless for too long.

So the truck spun on, winding north in the star-studded darkness, past the ghostly dunes of White Sands, north and then eventually east, to a narrower road, one that ran deep into the wrinkled land at the foot of the Guadalupes.

She made her way to the Crossroads by feel, and turned left without thinking. It was unsettling to be in a place so instantly familiar. The stars had come full out; the desert was bright beneath them. An ancient seabed, the Tularosa basin was now four thousand feet above sea level, and the air was thin, rarefied, so the starlight streamed through it undiminished. Amelia could see the beacon of the observatory to the south, high on the mountain, gleaming like a fallen star itself.

And then she was there, bumping the truck off the road next to the dirt lane that led to the house. The gate was closed. A new gate, one of those metal-barred affairs. Amelia left the truck idling when she got out, not sure it would start again if she turned it off after such a long run. But when she tried to open the gate, she found it padlocked. Her grandfather never did that.

She climbed up on the gate and looked toward the ranch house, sprawling among the cottonwood trees beyond the fields. No lights. No smoke from the chimney pipe. The windows were dark vacant blanks against the pale adobe walls of the house. She could see the looming windmill, its blades turning slowly in silhouette, but nothing else moved.

So maybe the ranch hadn't been leased to some-one else. Maybe her uncle hadn't decided she was dead and sold the place off. Maybe none of the things she'd been afraid of had happened.

She should have been relieved. But the homesickness was back, wilder than ever, and she realized that some part of her had expected her grandfather to be there waiting for her.

He was dead. Bound to be. He'd been seventy-six the last time she and her kid brother had come for the summer, and that was more than a dozen years ago. But one thing she had no doubt about—that Gramps had kept his word and left the property to her. She knew he had, as surely as she knew the pattern the cottonwoods' shadow would paint on the house in summer. This place was part of her.

She went back and cut off the truck. The silence was a living one, even in February. The rustle of a mouse in its nest and the faraway cry of a hunting night bird gathered on the wind. Amelia shivered. She put on her down vest, then took her backpack and her cooler out of the truck. Nobody would bother her things, not out here. Gramps used to say they could go a week without seeing another soul on this road.

He'd been exaggerating, of course. Something he was prone to. Amelia dropped the cooler over the fence, then swung herself over the gate. She picked up the cooler and started down the lane toward the house. The smell of the desert seemed even more sharply familiar now, thick with memories. She remembered racing Michael down this road on bikes—Gramps taking the two of them to collect native grasses by the old railroad tracks, Gramma baking biscuits in the cool of the morning. So many memories. A cascade of them.

They were falling around her like rain. Amelia bowed her head and walked up the road into it.

On sale in August:

AMANDA
by Kay Hooper

THE MARSHAL AND THE HEIRESS
by Patricia Potter

TEXAS LOVER
by Adrienne deWolfe